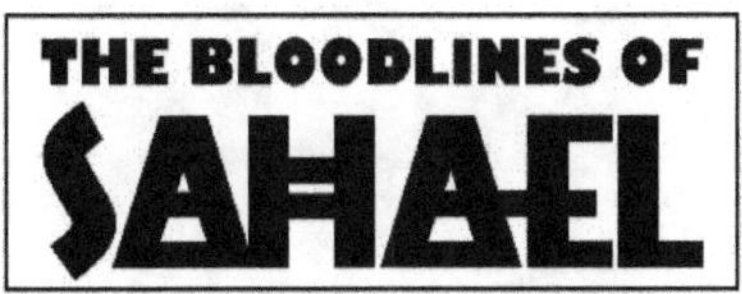

THE BLOODLINES OF SAHAEL

VOLUME TWO

BOOK FIVE

THE YORUBA OF SAHAEL

BY

DWAYNE ANTHONY MADRY

Printed in the United States of America

First Printing, 2025

Cover Design by JessHavok

ISBN 978-1-963089-43-1

www.SAHAEL.com

Intoduction into Sahael

As the sun dipped below the horizon, casting golden hues across the land, Aamira began her long-awaited journey back to SAHAEL. Accompanied by her steadfast family, she remained blissfully unaware of the trials and tribulations that awaited them on this fateful path.

For Aamira was no ordinary traveler; she bore the weighty legacy of the Black Madonna of the Yoruban Bloodline—a divine avatar of the Sacred Bloodline, chosen by the Creators themselves. Imbued with an unyielding power, she was destined to endure the fiercest storms and conquer the darkest adversities for the sake of her kin, her people, and the very fabric of her kingdom.

As she ventured forth, the air crackled with anticipation, a harbinger of the epic battles to come. With each step, she felt the pulse of Alkebulan and Aarde—the ancestral lands calling out for salvation.

In this grand tapestry woven by fate, Aamira stood as the beacon of hope, ready to unleash her strength and wisdom against the encroaching shadows. The realms awaited her courage, for she was not merely a protector; she was the embodiment of resilience, destined to reclaim her legacy and forge a new dawn for all.

CHAPTER CONTENTS

CHAPTER I
FREE WILL

N'eropoili, Nycea, Dameon's Manor

Rarely had Aamira worried about the odds against her. Since her childhood, armies and entire cultures had conspired to destroy her and her three cousins. War had been raged with the intent of murdering her, yet she had always survived. Her skill in battle had been tested many times, and she won the day each time.

This moment felt different.

She stood in the manor house of Damien, son of fallen angel Natas himself, on the island of N'eropoili where the armies of Natas resided. Only her husband Abioye, friend and Educator Adewara, and his daughter Lanae, stood by her side. It had been meant to be a secret spy mission to discover if Natas, or anyone under his sway, had gained the ability to create an unbeatable army of angry spirits. They had found evidence that Damien had indeed been delving into such arcane magic. Their discovery wouldn't matter if none of them made it off the island alive though.

And their chances of survival had plummeted in the past minute.

The sound of maniacal screams echoed through the ground

floor and up the stairs toward Damien's palatial bedroom where Aamira and her team stood in the dark. They had been discovered by the Nemods, insane witans, mutilated and covered in ash who would rape and murder indiscriminately.

Hundreds were now filling the house with the intent of killing the intruders.

The odds seemed worse than Aamira had ever faced.

"Weapons ready!" Abioye shouted. He and Aamira blinked her eyes twice, making them Zambian, and activating their Yoruban gifts. They manifested glowing green swords in each hand as Adewara pulled several throwing daggers from his belt.

"I only brought weapons of assassination, not battle," Lanae said as she stepped away from the door, and the sound of screaming beyond.

Aamira opened her mouth to respond when the door flew open and several bald Nemods, gray skin barely visible in the glow from her weapons, charged in with axes and saliva flying from their mouths. In response, she and Abioye leaped forward, cutting the insane attackers down quickly. All three fell dead, but before they had hit the ground, more rushed in. Adewara threw his daggers, killing several in the hallway before they could enter the bedroom. They fell dead, tripping up the Nemods behind them. The torches they had been carrying fell with them, setting fire to the rugs outside.

Aamira spun in a complete and continuous circle, slicing the Nemods in the room at the base of their torsos, detaching them from their bodies entirely. Abioye kicked several of the assailants out the door and slammed it shut.

"Help me hold the door!" he cried. Adewara and Lanae ran over and threw their bodies against the large wooden barrier.

Stepping back, Aamira felt warm blood between her toes as

she stepped in a puddle left behind by her dead enemies.

We can't win through sheer force, she thought quickly. Something else must be done.

She looked around the room. In the dark, few details could be seen beyond the statues of Damien that acted as pillars holding up the roof. The light from her weapon gleamed on something gold hanging on the wall, and Aamira saw a painting, seven feet tall in a golden frame, of Natas standing above Dameon with his hands on his son's shoulders. Natas's dreadlocks fell over his shoulders while Damien's afro caught the light of his glowing red eyes.

"Aamira!" Abioye shouted from behind her. "We can't hold the door much longer!"

Without looking back, Aamira came up with a plan. She hadn't skin-changed in 20 years, not since she trained her young sons in how to use that particular gift. She hated skin-changing, since it was incredibly painful and felt like the ultimate deception to oneself and the people around you.

Now was not a moment for such moral quandaries.

Staring at the painting, Aamira focused her energies on matching every detail of Damien's face and build. Warmth spread through her body, followed by intense agony. Her muscles shifted, bones extended, skin stretched. Aamira cried out as she doubled over.

"Aamira!" Abioye shouted. "Are you okay? Where are you? Help us hold the door!"

The pain subsided and she stood back up. She looked at her hands, now larger and masculine. There was no need to look in a mirror; she knew she was Damien.

"Open the door," she said, voice deep and melodic. She had never heard Damien's voice, but she doubted the Nemods had either, so a deep man's voice would have to do.

"Who said that?" Adewara asked, body pressed against the door.

"I've skin changed," Aamira answered as she stepped toward them. "Open the door."

Abioye's eyes were wide. "Aamira?"

"Open the door!" she bellowed.

Adewara, Abioye, and Lanae stepped back, allowing Nemods to crash into the room with their weapons, torches, and scarred faces ready to terrorize.

"How dare you enter my home uninvited!" Aamira roared, voice shaking the room. The Nemods paused, staring at what they assumed to be their master Damien. Fire burned in the hallway behind them as other Nemods continued rushing up the stairs.

"You come into my home and set fire to my belongings?" Aamira cried angrily, full of vengeance. "You will face the wrath of your savior and king, flesh burned from your bodies by my father, Lord Commander Natas!"

The Nemods, seemingly confused, began to cower and look at each other expectantly.

"Do you doubt your eyes?!" Aamira screamed. Her deep voice shook objects on tables nearby. "Do you dare defy your God? Would you desecrate this home in the name of your stupidity?!"

The closest Nemod dropped his ax and knelt shakily. The others followed. Soon, dozens of bald and mutilated Nemods chanted the name of Damien, son of Natas. The fire from their torches lit the room with a dancing red and orange glow.

"Come, my servants," Aamira said, motioning to Abioye and the others. "We will leave this place, and these wretches to their fate."

The Nemods moved aside as Aamira passed through them, followed by her team. Fire had begun to burn up the walls in the hallway. Heat radiated painfully.

Reaching the top of the stairs, Aamira looked down on the entry hall below, packed with confused Nemods. They looked pathetic and wretched. Life held nothing for them but murder and savagery. Whatever they had been before they submitted to Natas was lost to history. Now they were nothing but danger and pain wrapped in emaciated bodies. Death would be a mercy for them. And if it wasn't, Aamira didn't care.

"Burn the house!" she shouted. "Burn it now with all of you inside! That is the will of your God Damien! Sacrifice in his name!"

"Sacrifice in his name!" The Nemods cried. They began running through the house, setting everything on fire, including people close to them. Screams pierced the air as Aamira and the others ran down the stairs and into the courtyard beyond. Nemods flung torches into palm trees overhead and through the windows. As the spies fled through the front gate into the night, the manor of Damien burned behind them.

"That was genius!" Adewara gushed as they entered the grasslands. "I worried we had reached our end in that mansion."

Abioye hugged Aamira and then stepped back as if uncomfortable. "Sorry, it's just strange seeing you this way."

The house burned bright in the distance and Aamira felt they were far enough away to drop the façade. Releasing her energy, Aamira's muscles again burned painfully. Every nerve screamed at her. After a few moments, she slumped against Abioye, exhausted.

"I…hate doing…that," she gasped, once again in her true form.

"She has to rest," Abioye urged.

Adewara shook his head. "We need to make it back to the Nibiru Tunnel before dawn. The fire will draw the army, and they'll start searching the land like cockroaches. The Nemods are cowards. You saw what they were doing to each other as we left. Most of them won't sacrifice themselves even at the command of Damien. They'll burn each other first, and whoever is left will tell the Ennead soldiers that Damien commanded them to burn the house. The Ennead won't believe them, I would guess. We need to hurry."

As they ran through the night, a Nemod woman saw them in the grass and pursued. Abioye manifested a blade and easily killed her before she knew she was under attack. As her body lay there dead and bleeding out, it began to convulse violently.

"What's happening?" Abioye asked. "She's dead. Why is she moving like this?"

"When spirits leave the Narsan body, or anyone who has fully given themselves to Natas, it is trapped without anywhere to go, unable to travel beyond," Adewara said as the body continued flailing about. "They have given up their bodies for a cause that kills their minds and corrupts their spirit with white darkness. This is the reason why the white mist takes these wandering spirits to rest eternally in the skies as they wait to be awakened to help spread witan supremacy across Aarde. They join the Host, waiting to fight in Natas's army of the undead."

"You mean to tell me Natas would use his own kind as sacrifices to further his own agenda? Aamira asked.

Adewara nodded.

"So, these Nemods roaming the land are filled with nothing on the inside? They are spiritless bodies filled with nothingness?" Aamira asked.

"They have bound themselves through arcane magic to Natas and his cause. Their spirits have been rejected by the Eastern realm when the Nemods decided to give up their right of choice and free will. These Nemods sold their souls to a cause, so their spirits wander around in torment, until they're given purpose for their existence."

"Why?" Abioye asked.

"You would need to ask her," Adewara replied, pointing at the now still corpse in the grass. "We need to continue running. Ennead will collect this body soon enough."

Before sunrise they had crossed the grasslands and reached the city of Nith. Darkness still held sway, but the light of morning lit the eastern sky. The docile people they had seen wandering the streets the day before were all indoors sleeping, so Adewara led the team back to the sewer cover in the alley and underground. Before Aamira knew it, they had climbed down through the broken shafts and were inside the glowing tunnels that would lead them back to Inheritance.

Once safe in the Nibiru passages, Aamira collapsed. Deep breaths filled her lungs. Her entire body screamed at her to stop moving.

"She can't go any further," Abioye said, voice echoing in the tunnel. "I won't allow it."

"We can rest," Adewara agreed, also breathing heavily from their forced flight. "We're safe here. Let's set up camp and find some grubs to eat. I remember there was water dripping not far from here. I'll fill our skins and return."

Aamira was thirsty and hungry, but her fatigue conquered all those discomforts. She closed her eyes and fell into a dreamless sleep.

The next few days were a boring repeat of the last two months. They walked through the tunnels, digging for worms and large grubs to eat, finding water where they could, and then walking more. Aamira wished they had more time on the surface to eat a good meal before descending once again, but such things were not meant to be. No sun touched their faces in the tunnels. It was easy to become despondent, particularly with what they had learned about Natas's plans with the Host army.

"What do we do about Damien taking control of the spirits and creating an unbeatable army?" Abioye asked as they wandered through the shadows.

"According to what I've been reading in Damien's journals I took from his estate; they don't quite have the magic finalized yet." Adewara pulled one of the leatherbound books from his satchels and waved it. "There is a lot in these pages to digest. I haven't been able to read all of them in the last couple days, but what I have has confirmed much of what I had feared regarding many different things."

"Like what?" Abioye asked.

Aamira grimaced, knowing that such a question was an invitation for a lecture. Yes, she was bored trudging along in the tunnel for another day, but would one of Adewara's discourses make it better? She doubted it.

"In Katunkumene," Adewara began with his usual operatic excitement, "a council was called to discuss the inhabitants of Aarde. Ishtar and Obatala presented the proposition of Black Supremacy to the council to decide what should happen with the inhabitants of Aarde and the Ancient Kemites. The proposition for

Black Supremacy included every Black soul was to be blessed with the ability to choose for themselves and would be in the highest levels of government, finance, religion, education, and all things in Aarde. The Blacks were to show their love for all humanity and treat them all as equals."

"Sounds like a good plan," Aamira said.

Adewara opened the book as they walked. "It is. Even Natas supported the idea at first, according to Damien's writings. The plan was supposed to put Black people in every single position of power in Aarde to ensure that all things would be always done with fairness and merit."

"That's way better compared to what it is now: the complete and opposite idea of witan supremacy," Aamira replied. "All witans look out for other witans despite their mediocrity and worthlessness."

"And therein lies the problem of the idea of 'supremacy' as it is now understood," Adewara said. "Ishtar and Obatala's idea of supremacy was not one of sheer superiority, where one being is inherently better than others, but rather for administration. The descendants of the Kemetians had a greater capacity for good because of their status as being biologically closer to the realm of the Gods and thus would be given the administrative duties. The proposition for Black Supremacy provided the opportunity for all Obatala and Ishtar's children to return to their presence. Ishtar and Obatala provided them with the opportunity to make it happen."

"I can see how the proposition for Black Supremacy can be somewhat difficult to accept," Lanae said as she braided her hair. "One people being put above another has been so perverted in our world that we would think it could never function in the proper way. Nevertheless, Ishtar and Obatala provided a means for all people of all races to all return to their presence."

"How exactly?" Abioye asked.

"By allowing their Black children and witan children the opportunity to learn for themselves and to decide for themselves," Adewara continued. "The children from Katunkumene and the Ancients Kemites were both given the ability to choose a path for themselves, even if it was a path not approved by Ishtar and Obatala. To allow their children to return to a higher state of being after mortality, Ishtar and Obatala decided to provide a Black Messiah with wool hair and copper skin for the chosen bloodlines, the Ancient Kemites and the people of Aarde and Sahael."

"This is what Natas and Damien perverted," Abioye said, spitting in disgust.

"Exactly," Lanae replied. "And we saw it firsthand at the estate. Ishtar and Obatala want peace, growth, and intelligence. Natas wants servants who have mutilated themselves in his honor. I'd never seen anything like those Nemods before. They were tragic and terrible."

"Tell us who the Black Messiah was," Aamira said. She had heard about this gospel before, but seeing the contrast of Natas's plan up close on N'eropoili, the true plan became far more interesting to her.

"Horus, the second born son of Ishtar and Obatala after they denied their first son of the Morning Star, Natas," Adewara said.

Aamira nodded, remembering the first time she had learned of a Black Messiah at the Royal Rumble over 30 years ago. "Solomon said as much to my cousins and I in his tent during the fiftieth Royal Rumble. It was all so new to me then. I was only 18 years old at the time. I only half-listened. Oadira wanted us to run away and escape, and I pretended to want the same thing, but in my mind I longed to go back to the comfort of the plantation. I was so foolish. I thought only of myself. Even when the riots broke out, I still held to my selfishness. I'm glad I can listen now with a bit more maturity. And of course, getting a glimpse of a world controlled by Natas and Damien has made me rethink a lot of things."

"Does Damien give any of his perspective on the choosing of the Messiah since his father wasn't chosen?" Abioye asked.

"He does," Adewara confirmed, flipping through pages in the journal. "Surprisingly, it's a fairly truthful telling. He writes here, *'The council deliberated the proposition for Black Supremacy, the Black Messiah, and the Alkebulan union for months, according to my father. After months of debates, arguments, and compromise, Ishtar and Obatala decided that the savior of Aarde would be black and would be born in Alkebulan, not to be confused with the Middle East at all. Horus, the usurper-savior, was to be born in Egyptus and would grow up to be enslaved by his own witan brothers and sisters Enduring pain, suffering, and discrimination for all Black people persecuted and killed for no reason. Horus, the Black Messiah, would take on the burdens of hatred, systematic racism, and ethnic cleansing from his or her oppressors. It was foolish to follow this plan. My father was wise to realize this so early. May his glory reign for eternity.'"*

"Natas couldn't have been the only high angel to show opposition to the proposition for Black Supremacy," Aamira stated. "If he was as influential as the old records say, there must have been others."

"I'd like to know more about the opposition as well," Abioye said.

Closing the journal, Adewara took a drink from his water skin. "There was great opposition to Ishtar and Obatala's proposition. Lord Commander Natas, and one-third of Katunkumene's population opposed his parents' plan."

"The one-third," Abioye said, rubbing his chin. "I always forget about them. Natas gets all the mentions, but there were a huge number of spirits that followed him. He must have been persuasive as hell. I guess it makes sense. I mean, Ryland and Ryal are honorable witan men, and yet they were under Natas's sway for a time as well."

"Natas seemed defiant from the start," Aamira said.

"Not necessarily," Adewara explained. "Natas was given an opportunity to present an alternate proposition to the plan of Black Supremacy for Aarde. Natas came up with a slightly different version of the proposition. He wanted all Black people in control as well but wanted them to enslave every witan while promoting the sanctity of their own bloodlines. In his plan, Black people would rule unfairly in all things in government, finance, education, housing, ruling through dominance and oppression, just as the witans do now while under his influence. Natas wanted to take away the choice of free will to make his plan fool proof, nullifying the need for Horus to redeem every one of them for their sins."

"I doubt that went over well with the council," Aamira said.

"That's correct. It caused tension amongst the Katunkumene council." Adewara said. "But they continued to listen to Natas's alternate version of the proposition for Black Supremacy until he asked that the savior be witan, which would allow him the power to create a system of witan supremacy, and the construct of race, to help control and justify his treatment of witan people on Aarde. Natas's alternate proposition for Black Supremacy was rejected by the Katunkumene council unanimously, yielding not a single vote in Natas's favor. Last night I read Damien's description of the vote. Let me just say it was…colorful."

"I would've loved to have been there to see Natas's reaction," Aamira smiled.

"Lord Commander Natas stomped out of the council room

upset and motivated," Adewara said. "Again, Damien writes in great detail about his father's rage."

"So, the council meeting and the proposition for Black Supremacy took place after Nyathera's asteroid had passed over Katunkumene?" Aamira asked.

"Yes," Adewara answered. "The arrival of the Kemites to Aarde had already taken place via the asteroid impact. Aarde was ready for the spirits of men to come down into the bodies Ishtar and Obatala would create for them, but the Kemites were given their inheritance first. The asteroid passing Katunkumene prior to its impact on Aarde had unintended consequences, however. As Nyathera's asteroid passed over Katunkumene, millions of white jaded fragments fell all over the sacred sphere. The Katunkumene defenses sounded the alarm, alerting the celestial people to enter their homes until the fragments were disposed of properly by Katunkumene's defense systems. The holy people who disobeyed the warming and remained outside were rounded up and sent to the realm of outer Darkness."

"That sounds a bit harsh," Abioye said, almost tripping on a rock.

"This was the initial infection of White Darkness," Adewara replied.

"Wait, what?" Aamira said, stopping in her tracks. "I thought White Darkness was an influence, not an infection."

The others stopped as well. Adewara shrugged. "I had heard whisperings of this from other Educators. It was nothing more than theory. White Darkness is contained within each of the jaded pure white stones. These stones can change brain chemistry. Damien's writing confirms it. Initially, many Katunkumenes who knew they were infected did well in hiding, led by Natas, who seemed even then to understand the power that had accidentally infected the holy realm. Ishtar and Obatala knew they had to visit

Aarde to see the damage Nyathera's asteroid had caused. When they arrived in Aarde, their wraiths cleaned up the remaining jaded stone fragments. However, Natas's influence was at its zenith. He made sure to keep it a secret from Ishtar and Obatala as he snuck down without them even knowing to gather some of the stones. While on Aarde, he apparently heard Kaimana and Kainoa explain that the white jaded fragments were the stones of Khay and Hemiunu, their former leaders who had succumbed to the white darkness. Their spirits had been ripped out of their convulsing bodies to help further the Ukáváál bloodline. When the Ancient Kemites arrived in Aarde, Kaimana and Kainoa searched the entire planet for the Antikythera Mechanism that broke off and was lost, along with the Nimrud Lens, and special deposits of Damascus steel. It was later learned that Khay and Hemiunu secretly placed this infectious stone collection on Nyathera's asteroid in secret before their world was destroyed. The jaded white stones were used by the Ukáváál to control and manipulate the minds of their people. They were the cause of the destruction of their home world of Kolob."

"The fact that Natas was there without his parents knowing is tragic," Aamira said. "If only they had known, none of this would have happened."

"No, it's just the way of order," Adewara said.

"Please clarify," Aamira said, arms folded.

"There must needs be an opposition in all things. If not so, the proposition for Black supremacy could not be brought to pass, with neither dark whiteness, nor Black holiness nor misery, neither good," Adewara said. "Lord Commander Natas gained knowledge through his deception, but it is the natural order of things, promoted by Ishtar and Obatala, that such things happen in order for humanity to face trials and gain strength. The Ukáváál are the cause of the destruction of many worlds and may yet grow to power here. If blacks and witans are not strengthened, all will perish. Perhaps through pain and suffering it will come to pass that the Ukáváál may finally meet their end. This is why I follow the words of the prophets. I know, Empress Adesola, that you grow frustrated with my ways and faith. This is why I listen and wait, however. Histories are not told through a single person's lifetime, but through millennia and the tapestry of millions of faithful men and women working for a brighter day they may never see. I myself may never see that day, and I say so be it, so long as I am a servant of the greater good."

Nodding her head in understanding, Aamira felt a twinge of guilt that she had been so hard on Adewara, particularly about him not sharing the truth of being married with her sons. Adewara was a true believer, and the world needed true believers when things turned dark. She had seen that darkness in the eyes of the Nemods.

"I'm beginning to understand a bit better," she admitted.

"Was Natas infected by the stones too?" Abioye asked as he started walking again, urging the others to follow.

"Nineveh and Anubis found Natas, who had been infected with the stones as well," Adewara answered, stepping along with Abioye. "They loved Natas. Everyone did. That's something I've learned myself through deep study. He was beloved among all. They kept him hidden from the Supremes and the Divines in the realms of outer darkness. Anubis and Nineveh made sure to keep this devastating white mist locked away inside of them for all eternity. When Nineveh took the stones with her to the outer realms, she wanted to place the stone in the Nothing where only thought exists. Unfortunately, the white jaded stones were fragile and broke, infecting others. After returning to Katunkumene, Anubis and Nineveh were cast out because of their deception."

"There was a lot of casting out going on," Aamira chuckled mirthlessly.

"They knew better," Lanae replied. "Nineveh and Anubis too had become infected because they had let sin into their hearts. Those in the higher plains are held to a higher standard. They know all truth at once. When they cast off that truth for even a moment, they can no longer remain. Such is the natural order. It's not that Ishtar and Obatala want them gone; they have no more power over natural law than you or I do. Or Natas."

Adewara pulled a wriggling grub from his bag and chewed on it. "You speak true, my daughter. While in the outer realms of Darkness Anubis and Nineveh cracked open the Jaded stones. As they did, dark whiteness started spewing out of them, infecting their minds and the entire realm of darkness. As this took place, Lord Commander Natas worked in secret with his young son Damien who was to be an inside mole. The white darkness consumed their minds, infecting them to their core. This all happened prior to the presentation of the Proposition for Black Supremacy by Ishtar and Obatala to every Andalusian."

"How could Obatala and Ishtar allow this to happen?" Aamira asked. She thought about grabbing a grub from her own bag and eating it, but the thought of the bitter tang in her mouth made her hold out until she was starving.

"Ishtar and Obatala were unable to detect and feel the white darkness, in that it was a foreign substance that was full of hatred, death, and deception," Lanae said. "It was a concept they were unprepared to find in the hearts of their own children. Natas had begun to corrupt himself long before all of this, but the White Darkness amplified his ambition. He accepted the influence with all his heart."

"Ishtar and Obatala detected the white darkness after it was too late to do anything about it, which is why a civil war erupted in Katunkumene," Adewara added. "The Katunkumenes were immediately consumed by the white mist full of evil and superiority. The mist eventually found itself inside the emerald, sapphire, hematite gray, and turquoise locks that kept the four wicked generals imprisoned. Prior to the fall of Sahael, the four generals in Katunkumene were infected by this dark white mist. As a result, the sparks of rebellion transpired between the infected and the non-infected.”

“According to the records in Timbuktu, Katunkumene’s four generals were all six-star warriors undefeated in battles of any kind,” Aamira said.

Adewara rubbed his eyes as they walked past particularly bright glowing crystals. “The four Generals started convincing other Katunkumenes of the righteousness of Natas’s plan. They knew this wasn’t true. All of them had been taught the true ways and knew for a certainty what was right but chose to rebel anyway. Over the course of that time, one-third of the Katunkumene people were infected by white darkness. The four generals invited those who wanted to know more about Natas’s alternate proposition of Black Supremacy to join them in a feast. It is here that Natas arrived with Phylacteries full of white darkness to infect and control the minds of those in attendance.”

“Okay, wait a minute,” Aamira said. This talk of control had made her confused, and a little angry. “If all these powerful spirits were under Natas’s control because of the White Darkness, how could they be held accountable before Ishtar and Obatala? What you’re telling me is that if I were to come into contact with the White Darkness, I would lose control and be cast out forever. That’s not only unfair, but it’s unjust! I would lose my redemption because of the actions of another person.”

Slowing down, Adewara stopped once more and put his hands on his hips. “We should set up camp and have our evening meal as we discuss. Come, let’s sit and ponder.”

The ‘meal’ was nothing more than worms and grubs, which

Aamira ate for sustenance only. She gulped them down with a grimace on her face.

"What you say is true, Empress Aamira," Adewara continued after he had eaten a few worms. "Had the infected spirits had no choice over their actions, they would not have been cast out. In fact, many who were infected in the initial raining of the astral material were able to throw off its effects and return to their previous state in Katunkumene without incident or punishment. Many others, however, gave in to the feelings of pleasure and power the White Darkness provided. They chose to continue in rebellion that had already begun to foster in their hearts. It gave them an excuse to fight against truths they simply didn't agree with. They wanted to forge truths of their own regardless of whether they were completely false or not. You see, the White Darkness infected and influenced them, but like Natas, they choose their path themselves. Yes, many were deceived into becoming infected, but they then chose to allow that infection to fester in their hearts. They wanted power and authority, and if the true principles of eternity would not allow them to have it, they would rewrite false laws that would let them oppress and destroy to their heart's content."

Aamira sat, chewing on a particularly bitter larva. She had learned so much through the years of eternity, Sahael, and Natas himself. Adding to that knowledge always seemed to come with conflict. She understood only bits and pieces of the history all around her. Could she ever become like Adewara, perfectly content in the plan of his Creators, without doubt or question?

"All of this started an indoctrination process," Lanae continued where her father had left off, "in which Natas preached his proposition to those who would listen to him, causing the people in Katunkumene to flip to his side because they believed fervently the words coming from his mouth. As Natas's followers increased, so did his platform to speak to the Katunkumene people.

It all started out slowly, gaining influence, before Natas presented his proposition to Ishtar and Obatala."

"Over time Natas became a threat to his own parents who were advised to take out their first-born child," Adewara said.

"It seems this all could have been avoided," Abioye said as he washed down his meal with some water.

"Yes," Adewara nodded. "Ishtar and Obatala wanted to execute Natas, but they were counseled by Kaimana and Kainoa that their child needed to live so Natas could fulfill his purpose. Unfortunately, not killing their son led to civil war. One-third of the Katunkumene people became followers of Lord Commander Natas and were all cast into the three realms of outer darkness. Lord Commander Natas was thrown into the Nothing for all eternity."

"But we all know that didn't work, Adewara," Aamira replied. "Natas was still able to invade Sahael and disperse the bloodlines of the diaspora."

"Correct. Unfortunately, Natas found a way to escape the Nothing."

"How is it called 'the Nothing' if you're able to escape?" Aamira asked.

"No one knows except Lord Commander Natas himself. The Nothing is meant as a conceptual place where matter is broken down into thought and idea. Natas should not have been able to reincorporate his pure spiritual body, and yet, either by himself or with the help of Nineveh and Anubis, he escaped. After learning about their son's disappearance, Ishtar and Obatala sent down their chosen bloodlines to save the people of Kaimana and Kainoa, mingling with their ancient bloodline."

"We all know Lord Commander Natas is here in Aarde," Abioye said.

"Yes," Aamira said, leaning forward. "The last time I saw him was when I was with my cousins Oadira and Heziara at the Royal Rumble."

"Natas has been working in the shadows for centuries now," Adewara said. "His influence grows even now. Look at what we saw just a few days ago on N'eropoili. That is the world Natas wishes to create and perpetuate. And now he and Damien obviously believe they can imbue dead bodies with the spirits of the Host who were cast out with him. If that happens, Aarde will fall into darkness even deeper than what we feel now with the enslavement of our people."

"We need to find out what's happening," Aamira said.

Adewara opened another of Damien's journals and pointed to a page covered in diagrams of a drawn woman with wings. "According to these entries here, Damien has been experimenting with members of the Hausan bloodline. Their wings are systematically removed while their brains and bodies are tormented until they are killed. According to his writings, Damien has succeeded in some cases in allowing members of the Host to take control of the dead bodies of these poor souls."

"Heziara," Aamira whispered, thinking of her cousin.

"Yes," Adewara said, scratching at his beard slowly. "Heziara is of the Hausan bloodline. The Hausans are a people that possess the ability to fly. They are born with wings that as they grow to adolescence, allow them to soar. It is beautiful. They are a rare people who often hide their wings through magical means."

"And he used them to perfect his ability to place Host spirits into dead bodies," Aamira said, neck muscles tight. She prayed that Heziara was alive and safe.

"We should rest for the night," Adewara said finally. "We have a lot to think about."

Abioye pulled his sleeping pad from his back and laid it out, but Aamira continued sitting there.

"Where is Damien now?" she asked. "Do his journals say anything about that?"

"They do," Adewara replied as he spread out his own bedroll. "Naharis's Realm. That is where the Demirrians live. Lord Lieutenant Damien was able to infiltrate and take control of Naharis's realm apparently, cutting off all communications with Ishtar and Obatala. The laws of Death allowed Damien the opportunity to take control and harness the power of the dead to help run Naharis's realm. Again, this is according to his own writing, so whether it is fully true or not is hard to say. He and his father are not the most reliable individuals. Sleep for now, Empress. Get some sleep."

But Aamira couldn't sleep. Even as the crystals on the wall slowly dropped their light, she lay in darkness thinking about everything they had learned. How would they ever be able to defeat Natas and Damien? How could they stand against ignorance and oppression when so many people, both witan and black, choose both so readily? She felt as if what she had been asked to do was impossible. Even if Sahael was redeemed, how would they ever mount a force big enough and powerful enough to threaten Natas? He would soon command an army of the dead along with all the witan forces he controlled across Aarde on every continent and in every clime. How would they ever find victory against him?

Depression clung to her heart as she eventually fell asleep.

CHAPTER II
THE NIBIRU DETOUR

Aarde, Nibiru Tunnels, The Romans

"Are we lost? Aamira asked.

Four weeks had passed since their discussion of Damien's journals. For the past two days, Adewara had constantly stopped, checked maps, and looked at symbols on the tunnel walls as if he had lost track of where they were in this underground system.

"No," Adewara replied as he looked at various tunnel branches leading off into the darkness.

"Then where are we going?" Abioye questioned.

"We're on our way back to Inheritance," Lanae said as if in defense of her father. "However, I did notice that we passed a Roman sigil that was sealed off and made to look like a part of the tunnel yesterday."

"I saw it," Adewara said with a hint of frustration in his voice. He continued looking down at his map. "It was easy to miss if you weren't aware of them or told about them. The Roman sigil was that of a lion's head looking directly at you with its Carnelian eyes shining brightly."

"What did it mean?" Aamira asked. The last thing she

wanted was to hear they had taken a wrong turn in the tunnels and would have to turn back. She dreamed about seeing the sun again and eating real food.

"This Roman sigil was a marker for the Rysallian bloodline. Ryal told me before we left that we might see some of them in the tunnels. Many of his people went into hiding, especially the black members of his clan, after the fall of Sahael. They call themselves Roamers now."

As they continued walking, Lanae stopped and kicked at what looked like a few small stones.

"We need to be careful," she said. "I don't think we've been in this tunnel before. There are Treep droppings all along here."

"What are Treeps?" Aamira asked.

"Dangerous bioluminescent widow spiders the size of dogs," Lanae breathed, eyes now focused on the walls around them. "They roam these tunnels and devour anything if their cobwebs are triggered in any way whatsoever."

"Wonderful," Abioye whispered. He looked up at the dark ceiling, forming a knife in his right hand.

"If we haven't been in this tunnel before, then where the hell are we?" Aamira demanded.

"I'm trying to figure it out," Adewara snapped. He rarely got flustered, but Aamira could tell he was not happy with whatever mistake he had made in their navigation.

Lanae walked up to her father and put her hand on his shoulder. "Father, if this is a tunnel marked with the Roman lion symbol, there may be people here that could help us."

"What people?" Abioye asked, eyes still locked on the ceiling.

"The Roamers," Lanae answered.

"How would people live down here over long periods of time?" asked Aamira. "I know that Inheritance has the large crystals that shine light and allow plants to grow, but we haven't encountered anything like that in the tunnels. We've been living off beetles and larvae for god's sake. What would they be eating?"

"Sapphire, and Emerald lights illuminate these tunnels," Adewara replied, placing the map back inside his bag. "When life is detected, the lights point to where large bodies of heat congregate. When we arrive, they will be living in large tunnel pockets that were created by the Ancient Kemet's to hide if they were ever to face extinction."

"How did they even find this place?" Aamira asked.

"Solomon, the protector of Aarde, encountered them wandering through the D.I.M. T.I.M. Lands and wanted to help them. They were a dying bloodline. Not one witan would help them out of fear of retaliation from Lord Commander Natas. They were to wither away and die, but Solomon provided them with a way to preserve their culture, bloodline, legacy, and way of life. They were to emerge when the time was right. They have no royal lineage or leader."

"Ryal can lead them," Lanae said. "Ryal is the last of his bloodline, and they will follow him if they truly are leaderless. The Rysallian bloodline combined with the Black Roman bloodline will be formidable not only for Sahael but for Alkebulan as well."

"The question is, does Ryal want to lead them?" Adewara asked Lanae. "He is repentant of he and his father's mistakes and wants to help in the salvation of Sahael, nothing more."

"How do we even know if these Romans are not as violent as the other Rysallian remnants who Ryland and Ryal told us about?" Abioye asked.

"These Blacks Romans are not a violent bloodline, or at least they weren't." Adewara said.

"Well, that's encouraging," Abioye mumbled while shaking his head.

"So, what does this mean?" Aamira asked. "We took a wrong turn and now must find these Roamers so we can learn where we are? I want to get out of these damn tunnels and never enter them again!"

"I know," Adewara said, hand raised in a calming gesture. "And I'm sorry. I have no idea where we went wrong, so retracing our steps could take weeks. But if we travel a bit farther, we may be able to talk to these people and find a faster way out. And if they are violent, we can at least offer them news of the outside world that they may be willing to barter for. We have options."

"I'm glad you're so confident," Aamira scoffed.

"I understand the anger and frustration you feel, but now you have to put that anger and frustration aside and do what is best for not only your people but for your family," Adewara said candidly and boldly. "They are the same color as you and your people. They were enslaved and killed just as your family. They share the same bloodline and are the same. these Black Romans chose not to partake in a plan that would've killed and enslaved your people."

"I know that," Aamira said, angry to be talked down to. "I'm just saying that if they hid themselves away, we know nothing about their loyalties or culture at this point. As far as we know, they could consider killing visitors as the ultimate sign of honor."

"What you need to realize is there are six sacred bloodlines that need to return to Sahael," Adewara said. "Ryland and Ryal are the only ones of their bloodline that can return to Sahael. Despite my anger on the subject, they would not be violating the Nairobi laws. They wouldn't have been saved and preserved if they weren't pure in heart for the choices they have made. That is why I trust."

"These Black Romans could now be a part of the six sacred bloodlines, and there is good that can come from that." Lanae added.

"You're making a lot of assumptions here," Aamira said.

"I'm having faith," Adewara countered.

"That's your answer to everything."

"None of them have or share the same characteristics that the witan Rysallian bloodline once shared." Lanae said.

"Exactly," Adewara continued. "These Black Romans have not mingled with those who are racist. They have multiplied for good and have learned their ways. The Black Romans believe in a higher power. They may not know what that higher power is, but they believe. And with the right leader, they could help redeem Sahael. Ryal can help them understand that truth, giving them a purpose in Aarde by replacing the Rysallians. The more we talk about this, the more sure I am that our accidentally choosing the wrong path is in fact Ishtar's guidance. We were meant to come this way. I am sure of it now!"

Aamira thought for a moment as they continued walking. "I don't agree, but I can't exactly walk off on my own at this point. So, what's the plan if we run into the Roamers?"

"What you need to understand is that Romans come in different sizes, shapes, but one color: Black. Because of that, they are perfect for Sahael," Adewara said. "They're called Romans because they've roamed everywhere, never settling in one place, always moving. They wandered from one place to another, not creating roots: constantly on the move. Romans roam, living off the land, traveling and sailing the seas everywhere. One could say the Romans are the heartbeat of the world, knowing the ways of Aarde."

"If they roam so much," Abioye began, "then how do you know they're down here in the tunnels? In fact, how in the hell do you know so much about them?"

Adewara opened his mouth to answer but simply continued walking.

"Here we go," Aamira said angrily. "More secrets."

"No secrets," Adewara said, shaking his head defensively. "It's just that my daughter told me that residents of Inheritance have had contact with the Roamers many times over the past 50 years. There are large populations that come and go through the tunnels. Threads of our lives and activities are simply forming a tapestry in my mind, is all. I am understanding things to be connected that seemed unrelated. It is a singular experience for an Educator."

"I'm sure." Aamira said. "These Romans are going to be adopted and replace one of the six sacred bloodlines. That's basically what you've been getting at."

"Yes," Adewara said. He smiled and seemed overcome emotionally, but continued walking.

"Why?" Abioye asked.

"They will fix what has been missing," Adewara replied as a tear rolled down his cheek. "Ryal holds the true power within his bloodline, and through these Romans, we can graft them into the Marula Tree in Sahael through him. Although they meant well, the other lineages can no longer be trusted. Ibeji will prevent what we see as hereditary to manifest itself through them in future generations, and that is a chance we cannot take. I feel as though a giant puzzle piece has fallen into place, solving so many potential problems simply because I took a wrong turn. Praise Ishtar and

Obatala! Praise the Creators!"

A tingle moved up Aamira's spine. She had never felt the spiritual pull in the same way Adewara obviously did, but she couldn't help but be touched by his emotion. Adewara hid his feelings so completely that having him break down in joy in a shadowed tunnel because he felt the hand of the Divine in his actions, gave Aamira hope that perhaps they were indeed on the right path.

"Okay," Aamira began. "Let's say you're right and these Roamers are peaceful and excited to be grafted into the bloodlines. Ryal and Ryland are witan."

"This is why Ryal will be married to Black women," Lanae answered. "They are Rysallian and thus part of the chosen lineage, but any wives they take will need to be Black, ensuring that the chosen right of election remains within the Black bloodline permanently."

"How is all of this possible to replace one bloodline with another bloodline?" Abioye asked after a brief silence.

Adewara walked up to the closest wall and pointed at a symbol of a lion's head with its mouth open. "We're close! This is the Roman sigil. Praise the gods of Katunkumene!"

Smiling, Lanae fielded Abioye's question. "The answer to your inquiry, Emperor Abioye, is when a bloodline chooses to enslave another bloodline within the sacred six bloodlines, it can no longer be permitted. That bloodline must be eradicated, or it can no longer be allowed entry into Sahael. My father and I have spoken about this at length since your defending of Ryland and Ryal before the council of Inheritance. Despite their repentance, the possibility remains that they may once again try to overthrow those in power over them. Ryal I feel is genuine and cleansed of all pride, but Ryland was once a king. It is difficult for such men to purge themselves of their nature once power has been thrust on them.”

“You believe Ryland will sooner or later have such thoughts as to want to overthrow and control Sahael?” Abioye questioned.

“I’m not sure I fully believe that anymore,” Adewara said as he walked back to the others. “I have spoken with Ryland quite a bit during the short time we were in Inheritance. I believe he is free from his need to rule. However, we have thought that of people before and been betrayed by them. We will follow the laws of adoption to the letter. They both will marry Black women if they choose to have further posterity.”

Aamira clapped her hands together, surprised at how loudly the sound refracted in the tunnel. “I guess it’s settled then. We need to find these Romans and get them back to Inheritance so we can make our way to Sahael.”

“I agree,” Abioye grinned.

Placing his hand on Aamira’s shoulder, Adewara nodded his head. “Are you embracing your faith, Empress?”

“I’m embracing my faith in you. That will have to be enough for now.”

Hours passed. No sign of any side tunnels was evident, though the party began to see spiderwebs strung from the walls in greater numbers. The silky strands were limp and covered in dust, but evidenced the presence of the dangerous Treep creatures Adewara had warned them about. After another hour, the webs became denser, and they found several Treep carcasses covered in bioluminescent scorpions that fed on the carrion.

"I thought the tunnels were bad before we started finding the bodies of giant spiders," Abioye said.

Soon their passage became even slower, as fresh webs filled the path. They did their best to avoid them, but at one point, Aamira needed to cut several strands if they were to continue forward.

"Be watchful," Adewara warned, eyes shifting back and forth.

"I suggest we hurry and get to where we're going as soon as possible. Trouble is coming," Lanae said.

The tunnel scorpions started following them like a cluster of glowing lights.

"I'm going to assume that's not a good sign," Abioye said while staring at the scorpions.

"We need to be patient and prepare for a fight. We all need to use our gifts and get ready," Adewara said.

Aamira and Abioye blinked their eyes twice, making them Zambian. Energy surrounded Aamira as a protective covering.

Webs began vibrating all around them. Scraping sounds echoed from above and all around.

"They're here!" Aamira shouted.

Several massive spiders dropped in front and behind them, charging without hesitation. Aamira lunged forward with her glowing swords, slicing limbs and stabbing at thoraxes. Greenish-gray blood spattered the ground. More spiders descended. Scorpions advanced and tried to crawl up her legs, but she stomped them as best she could. Aamira fought with skill and speed, seeing Abioye and the others doing the same.

Still, already the spiders were starting to overwhelm them.

"We need to find a way out of here!" Adewara yelled.

More spiders scurried forward.

Suddenly the tunnel behind them lit up. Aamira turned to see two glowing eyes on the wall to their left. They looked like lion's eyes. The spiders hesitated in the light. A low-pitched sound echoed through the corridor like stone scraping against stone. As if frightened, the spiders leaped back and began climbing up their webs into the consuming darkness above.

A door opened, filling the tunnel with light. Aamira placed her hand in front of her eyes to keep from being blinded in the brightness.

"Ngozi's carnelian flame!" Adewara cried.

Aamira hadn't seen light like this since they had exited the tunnels in the city of Nith. Shadowed figures stepped out and rushed the four intruders. Before Aamira could react, she felt strong hands grabbing her.

"Get your hands off my wife!" Abioye yelled as he struggled against his own assailants.

"You are trespassing!" a deep voice echoed. Aamira couldn't tell who was speaking because of the light. "You will not make demands here! Surrender or be executed. We can leave you to the Treeps as well if you prefer."

"We surrender!" Adewara yelled. "We are not here to fight! Please, we can explain ourselves, if you'll let us."

Roughly, Aamira, Abioye, Adewara, and Lanae were pulled through the entrance into the light. As her eyes adjusted, Aamira saw that they were inside a cave. Much like Inheritance, crystals covered the high ceiling, somehow transferring the sun's energy from the world above. Buildings and streets filled the space. It was nowhere near as big as the cities of Iru underground on Inheritance, but it was still a more pleasant place than the tunnels themselves.

Hundreds of Romans crowded around curious as to why the gate had been opened. Aamira looked at the men who had grabbed them, seeing their dark skin and simple leather armor. They were strong and likely capable warriors.

"Look at her glowing sword," a young boy pointed. Aamira had not allowed her weapon to fade away, unsure what they would be facing.

"Her eyes glow green as well," an old woman whispered.

One of the warriors stepped in front of Aamira. "Who are you, and why are you in our tunnels?"

"She is the Black Madonna!" Adewara said loudly, as if to get the crowd's attention more than the soldier. "We were led here by Ishtar and Obatala. Our calling is to invite you to join us in the redemption of the holy city of Sahael and the entire Alkebulan continent!"

A murmur rippled through the crowd. People looked at each other and asked questions that all blended into one mass of sound.

The warrior who had questioned Aamira stepped back. "You have glowing eyes," he said, in awe. "We have been waiting…waiting for so long."

He stopped talking and instead knelt in front of her, head bowed. The other soldiers did the same, and the crowd followed their lead. Soon everyone Aamira could see was bowing to her silently.

"What is going on, Adewara?" Aamira asked as she scanned the area.

"They've been here waiting for our assistance," Adewara said with a large grin. "It's as I hoped. We've been led here by the hand of the Creators!"

"Where are we?" Aamira asked the soldier directly in front of her.

"The Roman sanctum," the man replied.

"The Sanctum has been a safe haven for us," a woman said, standing from among the soldiers. She wore leather armor like the men but had silver jewelry around her neck and wrists. She stood six-feet-five inches tall, with long black straight hair and chocolate skin, which magnified her beauty. A lion's head necklace graced her neck, and two rings were on her left hand. "My name is Caesar Rashida. I speak on behalf of those who have been mocked and spat upon wherever we go; those who were only looking for our home. When we were above land, and on the surface, we were never protected. This has been the base from which we have traveled. We beg you to spare our lives. We are unworthy of your presence."

"We aren't here to harm anyone," Aamira assured, concerned they would think she and her husband were a danger.

Rashida bowed her head. "I meant no offence. We have wandered for decades and know of the history of Aarde and how witans have treated Black people. These Blacks are the last of the Romans who understand they could be killed at a moment's notice just for being Roman. It's why the Romans have had to remain hidden for as long as possible to stay safe from those who would seek harm against them."

"I understand," Aamira replied. "But we would never harm you."

"We know our people ran away from the fight," Rashida continued. "We know our fathers brought shame on our heads."

"They were sent away by Solomon," Adewara said. "No blame is to be placed on you or your ancestors. You have submitted yourselves to Empress Adesola of the Yoruban bloodline. You are a non-Rysallian bloodline that can be grafted into the ancient lineage. Before you stand myself, Educator Adewara, my daughter Lanae, also an Educator, and our Empress and Emperor, Aamira and Abioye Adesola."

"The Signs of the Times are upon us!" Lanae shouted. People nodded their heads, but many seemed afraid to look Aamira in the eye.

Rashida bowed her head before looking over at Adewara. "You said something about being grafted into the sacred lineage. How is such a thing possible?"

"The Nairobi Laws allow for it," Adewara replied. "As long as one member of the sacred bloodline remains, they may bring another into the bloodline with the consent of the five tribes in Sahael. At that time, you will breathe of the orange carnelian mist. It will immediately change your eyes from brown to orange, alleviating the former Rysallians of their bloodline powers that will then reside within your Roman bloodline. The Black Rysallians will be required to mingle with you so that their children will have the added benefits of the Bloodline's powers once more."

Turning again to Aamira, a tear fell down Rashida's face. "You're the Black Madonna of your bloodline. The power, influence, and rights of your calling stretch back to the beginning of Aarde."

"They do," Aamira said.

"But we cannot follow you," Rashida stated.

"I'm sorry?" Aamira asked, caught off-guard.

Rashida stepped in front of Abioye. "We will follow him."

Aamira looked at Adewara. "What's this about?"

Adewara made a face that seemed to say, *'Listen and be*

quiet.'

She hated that face.

"All men of this world are capable of violence," Rashida said, staring into Abioye's eyes. "Especially the witan men who would rather kill than listen. They have their feelings hurt along with their sense of pride, never admitting when they are wrong. The Narsans have all been poisoned to think a certain way, and that way is why Black people have been enslaved, tortured, and killed for centuries. Because of this, our Sahaelian leader must be male. Only through this example of power and grace can we leave our sanctuary and roam no more. Without a male at our head, we will not have the respect of the other kings of Sahael, as we would not have the respect of the witan kingdoms."

Aamira rolled her eyes. These Roamers were following the same pattern as the witans. Still, as long as they followed Abioye, they would be safe and have an excellent role model. He would protect them against any adversary, even other rulers in Alkebulan.

"I understand," Abioye said, nodding his head in agreement. "Your people have nothing to worry about from the other Kings when you reach Sahael. I don't know how the other rulers will feel, but I will help them understand and approve of your grafting into the sacred bloodlines."

"You will be our authority on such matters," Rashida said. "With the consent of Empress Adesola, of course."

"My consent is granted," Aamira said candidly. The woman made it sound as if she was asking permission to seduce Abioye. He could lead them, yes, not sleep with this Caesar.

"Please sit down and rest for a while to eat and drink," Rashida said.

The group was led to a pavilion not far from the tunnel entrance where they sat at a circular table. After a few minutes, children ran forward with platters of fruits, vegetables, and even smoked fish. Aamira ate greedily, savoring the flavors. With each bite, gratitude filled her senses as she tried to forget the taste of grubs and worms.

This is a strange people, Aamira thought as she ate. *Adewara seems to think they're the answers to his unspoken prayers. Who knows? At least they have good food.*

The four visitors mingled amongst the Romans for several days, meeting with leaders and preparing the people to leave. As wanderers, they packed lightly and had no fear of leaving their homes. Their culture was built around the journey, which made them hearty travelers and quick to leave. No one seemed sad to be leaving the cavern. Aamira couldn't blame them though. Unlike the Iru cities underground on Inheritance Island, this town was smaller and claustrophobic. Buildings were tightly packed close together, with the crystals above sometimes less than 50 feet away. The cavern itself was far smaller than anything on Inheritance. All in all, Aamira wouldn't be sad to leave either. The good thing about the people being so organized was that they would have no problem taking advantage of the vacant cities on Inheritance. Even with 100,000 people, they would be able to sustain themselves in Iru easily enough.

On the evening of the fourth day, Adewara summoned Aamira and Abioye from their quarters in one of the stone apartment buildings to meet with the local Educator, Rufus.

"He will have detailed maps of the tunnels so we can get back to Inheritance faster," Adewara said as they entered the primary municipal building in the center of the city.

"If he can shave off even one day, I'll take it," Abioye said, holding Aamira's hand. "I miss my boys."

The group entered a small meeting room where Rashida and Lanae waited for them.

"Please sit," Rashida said, waving toward several worn chairs. "Educator Rufus will be here in a moment. He has educated us about the ancient bloodlines that were sent down to protect the Alkebulan people. Educator Rufus taught us about the atrocities committed against Black people due to the color of their skin and the resources their country offered. We were shunned and rejected by the witan bloodlines in Western Aarde above land. This happened because witans felt like they had been forced to treat us all as equals. The witan governments perceived this as a form of oppression and decided to fight against our progress and felt that enslavement had to be the solution. As Black Romans, we kept our faces covered to be protected from witans who would do us harm in Western Aarde."

"You have suffered as many of our kind have," Lanae said, placing her hand on Rashida's shoulder.

Educator Rufus then emerged from a door on the far side of the room. A tall man with brown eyes a black cloak, Educator Rufus wore the symbol of the Educators at the bottom of his gown. He had long gray dreadlocks to the middle of his back with ivory-colored teeth.

"I understand you are wanting to travel quickly through the Nibiru Tunnels," Rufus said with an almost indifferent tone. "There are multiple ways to travel and get to Inheritance to avoid the tunnel scorpions and the Treeps." He turned to Abioye. "My people tell me they are now yours to command and control; even our Roman militia."

"That is correct, Educator Rufus," Rashida said.

"The Roman people will be assimilated into Sahaelian society through the Rysallian bloodline," Abioye replied.

"Very good," Rufus said, continuing in his bored tone. "I have maps of the tunnels that will allow us to arrive in Inheritance in six weeks. It is the fastest route, though we will likely need to deal with Treeps and scorpions. Our population is 100,000 strong. Reports are coming in that everyone should be ready to leave by the morning after next. They would be ready now if not for preparations being made to guarantee this city and the animals and plants here are properly cared for. I would assume that moving through the tunnels with that many people all in one body will lead to us losing approximately one to two thousand people to sickness, attacks from Treeps, and scorpion bites. We can bury them along the way if needed."

He spoke so matter-of-fact that Aamira had to repeat to herself what he'd just said.

"So, you're saying between one and two thousand people will die on the way to Inheritance?" she asked.

"Yes," Rufus answered. "one to two percent. I've done the math. With a less prepared population, I would guess closer to five percent would die on the way. The tunnels can be quite dangerous, especially with large numbers of people making a ruckus."

"I won't let that happen," Abioye said, puffing out his chest.

"You will have very little power over the situation, despite what you tell yourself, Emperor Adesola," Rufus mused. "Leaders often overestimate their ability to keep their followers alive. It seems you are no different."

"And how many will die on the way to Sahael, do you think?" Abioye asked as if challenging the Educator's appraisal of the situation.

"I don't have enough data for such a journey. However, given rates of death from travel, attack, and disease, I would guess a further ten thousand."

"Ten thousand?" Aamira gasped. "You think we'll lose ten percent of the population going to Sahael?"

"Of course," Rufus shrugged. "Alkebulan is known to be a wasteland since Natas's destruction of Khartoum Palace. I think ten thousand is a conservative estimate, to be honest."

Adewara held his hands up to stop anyone else from protesting Rufus' numbers. "We're not here to litigate the safety of any one journey. We need to reach Inheritance and then Sahael. We will do our best to keep everyone safe. Once we're there, the bloodlines can be united through marriage. Caesar Rashida is the head of the bloodline. She will be united with Ryal, son of Ryland."

"What do you mean, 'united?'" Rashida asked.

"You will be married to Ryal," Adewara said.

Rashida blinked several times. "Why?"

"You're the Madonna of the Roman bloodline, and the man you will marry must be the Rex of the Roman bloodline." Adewara said. "You're going to be married when you all return to Sahael."

"No, I'm not," Rashida said, head shaking. "I'm only 20 years old. From what Lanae has told me, Ryal is 200 years old. I'm not marrying someone I've never met, let alone some old man."

"He actually looks young…" Abioye began.

"It's not how things are done in my culture," Rashida interrupted. "The woman chooses the man."

"And yet you need a man to lead you to Sahael," Aamira mumbled loud enough for her to hear.

"I won't marry someone I didn't choose," Rashida continued. "Especially not a witan man."

"You will for the sake of your bloodline," Adewara said as Rufus nodded along.

"Then so be it!" Rashida said, slamming her hands against the table.

"It's not as bad as it sounds," Aamira said, knowing what Rashida was feeling. "I married Abioye for these same reasons."

"But I am incredibly handsome, so why would you have not?" Abioye grinned.

"Ryal is handsome," Lanae smiled.

"All I'm saying," Aamira said loudly to cut off any more commentary, "is that love can foster in arranged marriages. I had feelings for Abioye, but I wasn't ready to be married to him by any means. I did it for the good of my people. And while our marriage has not always been one of unity of mind and body, we have come through it stronger and now more in love than ever before."

Rashida stood silent, staring at Aamira. The empress could say nothing to assuage this woman's fear and anger. Better not to say anything else.

Rufus turned and started walking back the way he came. "I'll alert the people that the plan to leave the day after tomorrow is still in force. I will see all of you then."

He walked out, leaving an awkward gathering behind.

As promised, the Roamers were ready to leave on the

morning of the second day. The city emptied. 100,000 people waited quietly by the main entrance to the Nibiru Tunnels as if packing up their life and moving on was something they did every other day. Most of the men and women carried packs filled with food and nothing else. No personal effects were needed, as their culture had grown accustomed to having nothing superfluous in their lives. Only the people around them mattered.

Aamira and the others were to lead from the front while the people would be protected on the rear by the Roman praetorian guards. These praetorians were elite fighters, capable of handing out untold amounts of damage.

"The Praetorian guard will follow your orders until we have found our home," Rashida said to Abioye as they entered the tunnel and followed Educators Rufus and Adewara into the shadowed system. "As for now, the Praetorian will take orders from only Emperor Adesola as to not disrupt the power structure in Sahael."

Aamira remained quiet, walking behind her husband and the beautiful Caesar. It would be Aamira and her cousins that would rule in Sahael, not any men. Still, she would allow this people their sexism so long as they fought for the cause of freedom and equality.

"The Nairobi Laws are to keep the Sahaelian house in check per Solomon's orders," Rashida noted. She walked close to Abioye.

Her youth bothered Aamira. Not that she worried about Abioye being unfaithful, it was just that Rashida had so little experience leading her people. They wandered around the world, yes, but a 20-year-old did not have the maturity to fight and die, to sacrifice everything. Aamira certainly hadn't at that age. But then she thought of Oadira, who at 18 years old had plotted with her and Heziara to escape the plantations and run away. Oadira never wavered. Oadira's bravery transcended age.

Where was Oadira right now? Was she fighting somewhere? Had she made it to Sahael and now prepared the way for others? If anyone could do it, Oadira would be the one.

"The Praetorians will be used as Khartoum's army to protect the twelve bloodlines," Abioye said as he continued talking with Rashida. "They will be separated into fourths assigned to each of the four kings to overrule the council with force if they have to for the sake of Aarde, Sahael, and Alkebulan."

"It makes sense," Rashida agreed.

Adewara turned his head toward the conversation as they walked. "Once the chosen right of election is yours, Rashida, You will consult with the four kings and queens to ensure that Sahael is always doing what is best for the people. This is a powerful role, and you will need to work with myself, Rufus, and Lanae to make sure such power doesn't corrupt you."

"I understand."

"The Praetorians will be the only ones allowed inside Khartoum palace when they arrive in Sahael, to ensure that the ancient families can feel safe at all costs." Adewara said.

"When we arrive, where will my people live?" Rashida asked, still walking very close to Abioye. "My hope is that they're not mocked, scorned, or treated unfairly because of the actions of our fathers."

"The Romans will be allowed to mingle with the people in each of the four cities inside of Khartoum Palace," Adewara answered. "The Romans will not be isolated in any way whatsoever. They'll not be allowed to live on their own or in their own personal communities; that will be forbidden."

"Solomon, the protector of Aarde, has a plan for you and your people," Abioye said.

"What plan is that?" Rashida asked. "What if we don't like the plan? What if the plan isn't fair?"

"Once you've all been brought into Sahael, there are rules and stipulations you and your people will have to follow," Rufus said without looking back. "Or you can continue wandering and roaming the land. It will be your choice. Otherwise, according to the laws and records we Educators hold dear, you 'll be seen as equals."

Rashida looked at Abioye and smiled. "We submit to these rules and will be loyal to Sahael for all time."

With so many people in the tunnel, attacks from Treeps became a daily occurrence. Scorpion bites plagued the refugees. Aamira quickly lost count of how many spiders she had killed. Every night Praetorians from the rearguard would bring sickness and casualty tallies. As Rufus had predicted, the numbers ballooned.

After six weeks, the Roman Educator announced they were drawing close to Inheritance. Not five minutes later, Treeps descended from a collapsed portion of the tunnel roof and attacked. Aamira conjured her blades and sliced through the arachnids. Praetorians rushed beside her, as did Abioye. The people backed away, never crying out in fear. Warm yellowish blood ran down Aamira's arm as she plunged her green sword into the web sack of one of the larger Treeps.

"Push forward!" Aamira cried. "We're almost there!"

The fighting intensified as if the Treeps and scorpions

knew the population approached their haven. A glowing symbol caught Aamira's eye on her left. The marula tree shone in the dark, revealing the circular orichalcum door that she and her team had left from over five months before.

"We're here!" Adewara shouted as he sliced the legs out from under a five-foot-tall Treep.

Scorpions swarmed all around beneath Aamira's feet. She stomped on them, but more scurried to bite.

We need to get inside, she thought desperately. Closing her eyes, Aamira imagined her four sons working in the fields of Inheritance, talking to local farmers about harvesting under the crystal sky. Was the image real, or merely her hope? She didn't know, but it gave her an idea.

Yekú, Yomí, Yemí, Yinká, she thought, trying to telepathically contact her sons from a distance. *We need your help at the gate to the Nibiru Tunnels. Hurry.*

She felt no response.

Even so, within minutes, the doors opened, and her boys rushed through, manifesting their weapons and slaughtering Treeps left and right. Other soldiers of Inheritance flooded through the entrance as well, shouting the battle cry of the underground people.

"Derinkuyu chini ya ardhi!"

The battle ended as quickly as it had begun.

"Mother!" Yomí yelled with a broad smile. He rushed over and gave Aamira a grand hug. The other boys embraced her as well, joyful at her and Abioye's return.

"We thought you would be coming back with information about the Host," Yekú grinned. "Instead, it looks like you brought half the population of Neros's Realm with you. I'm not going to be able to cook for so many people!"

Abioye swatted his son on the shoulder and chuckled. "We stumbled upon a few Roamers along the way."

The boys led the leaders through the tunnel as the population followed.

"There are too many people for Inheritance to feed," one of the guards whispered to another.

Even so, everyone was able to enter Inheritance and close the gate entrance behind them. Sunlight shone down from the crystal ceiling, warming Aamira's face after the darkness of the tunnels. It wasn't real sunshine, but she would take it.

Residents of Inheritance gathered as the massive flood of people filled the streets leading to the municipal center. Aamira noticed people pointing at the newcomers, worried looks on their faces. Many whispered "Roamers," as they passed.

Aamira walked over to Adewara as he led the population forward. "The people of Inheritance look concerned. They seem to know these people are Roman."

"The Lysinnians have a troubled history with the Roman bloodlines," Adewara replied. "Don't worry. I warned Rufus and Rashida about this. They know what to do."

Adewara and the leaders arrived at the central municipal buildings of Inheritance. They walked up the steps and turned to the crowd of Romans behind them. It seemed like the entire city had come to see what was going on. There had to be close to 150,000 people in the central city now with the addition of the Roamers. Members of the Iru council rushed from the Niriru Palace, shock evident on their faces.

"Who are these people?" Councilman Saulren asked frantically as he clutched at his white ceremonial robes.

Adewara and Lanae stepped forward.

"These are the remnants of the Roman bloodline," Adewara said with a bow.

"There must be tens of thousands!" another council member blurted.

Rufus took a step up the stairs. "I am Educator Rufus of the Roman people, council members, and according to my tally we have 98,243 Roman citizens here with us who survived the journey through the tunnels." He turned toward the crowds and raised his arms. "And we come in peace!" he shouted.

The Romans lifted their swords and axes above their heads before dropping them to the ground. They then bowed in one gesture and held their hands in the air as a symbol of their surrender.

Councilman Saulren shook his head, braided gray hair swishing over his shoulders. "That is almost twice the population we have here in Inheritance. The strain on the food supply alone will be devastating."

"They are here with us under Yoruban protection," Aamira said to everyone. "And everyone will eat. They have brought rations with them that were not consumed on our journey, and they have already agreed to serve in the fields to help sustain themselves. And the surrounding cities are vacant, so they will not affect housing either. We've had time to think this through."

"What's going on?" a voice shouted from the palace entrance. Ryal came rushing down the steps followed by his father Ryland. "Who are these people?" Ryal asked.

"The adopted bloodline that is being grafted into the sacred bloodline," Adewara answered. "They're replacing your former ancestry that has been removed from the sacred six lineages."

"How is this possible?" Ryal asked, pulling on his ear. "We are repentant."

"You're the last of your bloodline and need a new heritage to call your own," Adewara said. "The previous bloodline has lost the right to ever return to Sahael."

"But I thought you were going to fight for us," Ryland added.

"The Nairobi laws forbid it," Adewara said sharply. "Do I need to go over it with you again?"

"No," Ryal said, hanging his head down low.

"According to Nairobi Laws," Adewara continued, "as long as one member of the six sacred bloodlines is alive, after an act of defiance toward another bloodline, they must relinquish all claims to vacate their place, blessings, powers, and rights. They then leave only one heir, male or female, to merge with a new bloodline to be added to the five previous lineages."

Aamira approached Ryal and his father. "This is how we're fighting for you. This is how you are redeemed and will be able to once again enter Sahael. Do you understand?"

Ryal nodded and smiled sheepishly. "Yes."

"It will be accepted and approved by the other bloodlines," Aamira nodded. "My sisters will defer to my judgment on this matter and trust me, as will their husbands, I have no doubt."

"So, what do we do next?" Ryal asked.

"We need to prepare a marriage promise for you and Caesar Rashida here to be executed when you all return to Sahael," Adewara said candidly, pointing to Rashida.

Blinking rapidly, Ryal looked from Adewara to Rashida and back.

Aamira shook her head. Adewara had absolutely no bedside manners to speak of.

"Again," Aamira said, touching Ryal's arm. "This is how

we fight for you. As the heir of the Rysallian line, you will marry Rashida, the heir of the Roman line. They will be grafted into the Sahaelian population, and the Rysallians will be merged with them, thus allowing both people to take their rightful place in Alkebulan and the city of Sahael."

A deep breath blew from Ryal's lips as he looked at his father.

"Sacrifice is necessary when seeking forgiveness," Ryland said to his son while placing his hands on the man's shoulders. "Your mother taught us that, didn't she?"

"She did, Father," Ryal replied. He turned to Adewara. "I accept this marriage proposal, if Caesar Rashida will have me, that is."

Rashida looked at Abioye quickly before taking a step up the stairs toward Ryal. "I have already given my consent to this union," she said as if pre-rehearsed. "I accept the covenant and will unite with your people for the good of Aarde."

A smile pulled at Ryal's lips. "Then I consent as well. We will be united in Sahael. May I serve you in times of joy and sorrow, beautiful Rashida."

Lucky Ryal, Aamira heard Yemí say telepathically to his brothers. *I'd get engaged to her any day.*

I'd be married to her for a single night if needed, Yekú chuckled.

Be respectful, boys, Aamira replied.

Sorry, Mom.

"This is good," Adewara said, pulling Aamira's attention back to the newly betrothed couple. He turned and began addressing the gathered crowds. "We must prepare to empty Inheritance and travel to Sahael. The time has come! Tomorrow evening, we will perform the official betrothal chant. In the meantime, word must be spread that the prophecies are being fulfilled as we speak. The Rysallian bloodline has returned. The Romans are being grafted in. The daughters of Sahael are calling upon their power. Spread the word! We leave for Sahael! We leave to reclaim our homeland! We follow Empress Aamira to the glory of Ishtar and Obatala!"

The people cheered, vibrating the air itself with their shouts. A chill ran up Aamira's spine. For thirty years she had longed to set foot on the Alkebulan continent and enter the holy city of Sahael. Now that it approached, she felt trepidation. Was she ready to lead this people to a poisoned land? Would she be up to the task of fulfilling her role as a savior of the people?

Everything became real in that moment.

Whether she was ready or not, the time had finally arrived.

Preparations were well underway by the following evening for the journey to Sahael. During Aamira and Abioye's many months traveling to and from Nycea, their sons had not been idle. Yekú, Yomí, Yemí, and Yinká, had sailed with Admiral Abdul and four hundred men back to Timbuktu, gathering as many ships as they could from the docks inside the cave. They had only returned to Inheritance two weeks before, bringing with them dozens of ships, while recruiting others along the way. The Nibiru Wall had fallen back into the hands of the Narsans, but so many of the soldiers had been conscripted into the army by Natas for fear of Aamira and her cousins, that the trade route gates were almost completely unmanned. Ships passed through without inspection, allowing a fleet of ships to return to Inheritance.

That night, after a sumptuous dinner in the municipal hall that Aamira thoroughly enjoyed, Adewara stood with Ryal and Rashida before the Council of Iru to pronounce their betrothal. Ryal wore white robes with orange symbols woven up the arms, while Rashida wore the ceremonial armor of a Roman Caesar.

"Ryal and Rashida, repeat after me," Adewara said, arms outstretched. "The six promises that make a marriage: I will love and cherish you."

"I will love and cherish you," Ryal and Rashida repeated, holding hands and facing each other. Aamira couldn't tell if they were happy or simply content that their engagement would allow both peoples to join the journey to Sahael. She could see a spark of attraction in their eyes, but whether that would blossom into love was anyone's guess.

"I will stick by your side for Better or For Worse," Adewara continued. The couple repeated each phrase when given. "I'll be here for you in sickness and in health. I'll be by your side for richer or for poorer. My commitment to you means I'm forsaking all others. I'll be by your side until death do us part."

After Adewara said the six promises that make a marriage Ryal, and Rashida repeated his exact words.

Adewara nodded his head and turned to the gathered dignitaries. "The two of you are bound and betrothed forever as you wait to be married when we all return to Sahael. Then you will consummate your union and become one flesh, giving children to your new bloodline and the glory of Ishtar and Obatala."

After the festivities, Aamira, Adewara, Abioye, and Lanae met in one of the conference chambers beneath a glowing crystal filling the small room with orange light.

"We need to make our way to Nibiru lake and take the

Nibiru river on the other side of Eastern Aarde," Lanae said. "The ships will be ready within three days. The Roamers have been helping the people of Inheritance prepare for the journey. I must admit, they are masters at travelling light."

"They've had to be," Adewara nodded. "And supplies?"

"The Iru Council approved the removal of all food stores from the granaries and their relocation onto the ships," Lanae replied. "We're anticipating the journey to Alkebulan to take several months, and after that, we have no idea what food we will be able to find, so we are taking everything we can."

Aamira leaned against a table along the wall and breathed deeply. "Three days. And after that, our next stop is Alkebulan and then on to Sahael. It's hard to believe the final leg of our journey is finally upon us after all these years."

"Everyone will be prepared to embark on the ships," Lanae assured. "Every single Roman and Lysinnian. There is enough room for everyone on the ships your sons and Admiral Abdul gathered. They truly accomplished a miracle while we were gone."

"They knew of the Signs of the Times," Adewara said, eyes looking at the floor. "I had no doubt they would rise to the occasion when the gods whispered their need."

"They had a good teacher," Abioye said, seemingly aware of Adewara's pain at his estrangement from the boys.

"I hope they will agree with that statement someday," Adewara replied.

"Ryal and Rashida are now promised to each other for time and all of eternity," Lanae continued as if not caring about her father's psychological pain.

"Ryal seems happy and sad at the same time," Abioye said.

"It makes sense," Aamira shrugged. "He knows he is now

the last of his bloodline, and no other bloodlines will come from his Rysallian lineage. Ryal and the Romans are officially one of the six sacred bloodlines thanks to the Ngozi's flame."

"Yes," Adewara said, looking back up at the group. "They will inherit the powers and gifts of the bloodline that Ryal's kinship has given them. The Romans will be blessed with echolocation, linguistics, and loyalty, as their eyes begin to change ever so slightly to look like the eyes of Ryal. Rashida is young, but Ryal is two centuries old. They will need time to grow into a true Caesar couple and lead when the time comes."

"For now, we should rest and prepare ourselves for another long journey," Lanae said, stepping toward the door. "In three days, we set our sights on Sahael, or death."

Sahael or death, Aamira thought. *It seems like my entire adult life has been on that trajectory. Which one will I embrace when the time comes? Only the gods know.*

CHAPTER III
THE NAUTICAL TRADE

Aarde, Nuberran Sea, Nautical Triangle

Three weeks had passed since the armada had set sail from Inheritance. Admiral Abdul had trained the individual captains on the nautical patterns they would need to use in order to make it through hostile seas. The fleet was to remain in one line as if delivering goods and cargo. Every ship would have to travel within the circular trade and not deviate in any way to avoid drawing any more attention to them. The size of the convoy would give raiders pause, but Narsan ships might still make a fuss if they felt something was amiss. Keeping everyone's heads down and focused on not making too many waves was the smartest option.

Aamira stood on the deck of the lead vessel; the same one they had used to sail from Timbuktu. Instead of a handful of sailors acting as crew like during their first journey though, over three thousand people were crammed in every corner of the massive ship. Accommodations were tight, as they were on every ship in the armada.

Mist blew into Aamira's face as she looked at the overcast sky. The boat bounced slowly up and down beneath her feet as the ocean slammed against the hull. Admiral Abdula waved at her from across the deck, motioning for Aamira to join him in the captain's quarters for a meeting. She entered the space, seeing bedrolls all over the floor. Adewara, Abioye, her sons, and the admiral all stood around a table looking at maps and other documents.

"Empress," Admiral Abdul said. "We're traveling exceptionally fast on these winds and currents, which is good and bad. We are entering dangerous waters, and from here we'll be facing obstacles in the water and on land if we draw too close to shore."

"How can we avoid these obstacles? Aamira asked, looking at her children and husband.

"The obstacles are impossible to avoid," Adewara said. "There's no way all these ships will get through unscathed. It's practically going to be suicide for some of the vessels, if I'm reading the maps right. We're looking at jagged shoals that pull the currents toward them and leave ships completely smashed."

"Perhaps, the other ships can skip by those areas," Aamira implied.

Abdul pointed at the map. "There's no other way through except from the top near the Vannadale colony and then join in the rotation after that toward Lucedale."

"We need to be extra careful," Adewara said. "There are multiple fortresses set up on the water banks where they allow several ships to pass through at a time. They can be inspected individually for the proper cargo and goods, just like they did at the wall before we took control."

Aamira swallowed, knowing what 'cargo and goods' Adewara spoke of. "You mean slaves, precious metals, and food, right?"

Nodding his head, Abdul pulled out another map, this one with ocean currents marked in fading ink. "As we move through the circular trade, we will have to pick up goods of our own and then place other items on the ships to be dropped off elsewhere. Remember, we're pretending to be a trade flotilla. We must play the part."

"What types of goods will we be picking up?" Yekú asked. "Surely not slaves or anything like that."

"All manner of goods going to western Aarde pass through this location," Adewara answered. "We'll focus on things we need or can trade, like soil, water, things like that."

Yekú nodded. "If you could get me some fresh meats and maybe some peppers, I can cook up some good meals with the kitchen crew. I've been teaching them some culinary tricks that everyone will really appreciate."

"Can we get back to the slaves, please?" Yemí asked, arms folded. "We need to find a way to disrupt this trade system permanently. No one should be enslaved, and if we can stop it, we should."

"That is a discussion for when we have reclaimed Sahael," Adewara replied.

Yomí shook his head. "Why? We have one hundred thousand people with us in this armada right now, crammed on these ships. We could take any port we wanted and right some of these wrongs immediately."

Adewara looked at Aamira, but she simply tilted her head as if in agreement with her sons.

"I know our relationship has been…strained of late," Adewara said. "But I hope you princes have enough trust in me to know that I want the same thing as you. It's just that everything must be done at its proper time. Yes, we have a massive force with us, but if we don't return Sahael to its glory, any victory we achieve will be a temporary one at best. Please, trust me on this as you once did."

The princes grumbled but seemed satisfied with Adewara's explanation.

"Sahael or not," Abdul continued, "we have bigger problems to worry about right now. When they return, the Triennium will change up their sailing patterns to reveal ships that shouldn't be here."

"What happens to the ships that are caught out of pattern?" Yekú asked.

"They're confiscated and all their cargo is taken away immediately," Adewara explained.

"What about the crew?" Yomi asked.

Abdul scratched his cheek. "That's the problem. We have more people on board our ships than we should. By a huge margin. If any of us are boarded and word gets out, Narsan ships will be called in. Our weapons are few. Normally the crews will be placed in obsidian chains until they can explain their mishap. Once cleared, the crew is sent back to the Triennium lands to be claimed by their families. We will not receive such comfortable accommodations; I can assure you."

"What if crew members have no family in those lands?" Yemí asked.

"If it turns out that they don't have families, they're listed as spies and are dismembered and fed to the pigs," Abdul answered.

"Savages," Aamira said, thinking of how degraded the witan cultures had become.

"This is the first time I'm hearing about these Triennium,"

Abioye said, kicking a bedroll aside and pulling over a chair to sit down. "Please educate us about these witans."

"Gladly," Abdul replied. "The Triennium operates and rules the waters of Aarde, possessing one of the most potent fleets ever known, especially in Eastern Aarde. They have an agreement with the Trinity to transport all cargo to the west."

"Witans want to control everything of necessity," Aamira said.

"The witans in Western Aarde value the infinite resources of Alkebulan," Adewara said, leaning over the table. "This is why they built obsidian walls and established entrances into the waters around the continent."

"Adewara speaks true," Abdul agreed. He pulled out another map, showing the landmass of Alkebulan. "The ships can enter the Nautical Trade circle through Kumasi city and the Ruad Pass. Afterwards you must dock and depart your ships at Darth. This will lead you to a secret underground entrance to the Isle coast."

"What's the problem?" Abioye asked.

"When we arrive, we'll then have to capture several more ships to help spread out our population and transport all of us to Sahael," Adewara said. "If we are led by local ships with the right documentation, the rest of our fleet should be able to pass unmolested. On top of that, we'll need to force someone to tell us the current nautical maneuvers so we can continue on our way without drawing the attention of the Triennium commanders."

"How long will it take to move through the Nautical trade?" Aamira asked.

"This process takes at least a month before the other ships arrive and the patterns have changed, allowing ships the time to move through Ruad Pass and the nautical trade without disrupting the current routine," Abdul said.

Just then, the door flew open and one of Abdul's sailors ran in.

"Admiral!" he shouted. "A Triennium ship has come up beside us and is hailing using hand signals."

"Show me!" Abdul said as he charged out of the cabin. Aamira and the others followed.

A drizzle of rain had begun to fall as Abdul rushed to the starboard side. Just as the sailor had said, a ship had come alongside the large Timbuktu vessel. Black tar covered the smaller ship, with ornate white sails catching the wind. Two other similar ships approached as well, cannons locked and loaded, pointing directly at them

"We're going to be fine," Adewara said, stepping next to Aamira as she looked down at the enemy crafts.

"How are we going to be fine?" Aamira asked.

"Look," Adewara whispered, pointing at Abdul. The admiral moved his hands and fingers expertly, making symbols Aamira didn't recognize. The opposing captain responded with similar gestures.

"Abdul knows the seven patterns the Triennium use and how they will change their call signs," Adewara whispered. "This allows us to enter into the Nautical Trade and move through it effortlessly without being detected and bringing any unwanted attention to ourselves."

"At least for now," Aamira replied.

Abdul finished making his hand gestures and turned toward the people gathered on the deck. "Everyone remain calm and steady."

After a moment, a horn blew on the adjacent boat, and they

pulled away. The approaching ships veered off.

Aamira took a deep breath. "Does that mean all the ships are free to go?"

"They accepted my explanation," Abdul replied. "I communicated that we are a flotilla moving swiftly from Nycea toward Vannadale with a massive load of slave laborers. Since the only fleet large enough to command this many ships would be Dameon Son of Natas, they didn't ask too many questions. We're now on a charted course that has to be tightly followed. I'll send signals to the commanders on the other ships to follow my lead. We'll still need to learn the maneuvers after we get through the Ruad Pass if we hope to make it any farther."

The ship sailed toward the gate; a natural pass formed by towering red rock cliffs that tapered toward the water like a gigantic 'V.' Buildings covered the canyon walls and shoreline, most seemingly made of red concrete and stone. Rain continued to fall, leaving a depressing mist over the entire area.

Aamira noticed Triennium forces on the shores walking along as if following the boats as they moved through the Nautical circle. She also saw thousands of slaves being watched by armed Trinity forces. The black people wore rags and were catching fish, cleaning clothes, or being harassed by witans. An entire legion of troops stood half a mile away surrounding a hill where the Ruad Fortress sat with its red rock walls.

Every ship that sailed through the Ruad Pass was loaded with all kinds of goods essential to traveling to the next phase of the Nautical circle. Throughout the process, the path grew narrower as the cliffs drew closer on both sides.

"We'll be boarded in a few minutes," Admiral Abdul said to Aamira as they sailed toward the docks.

"What happens when the witans find our ship filled with

nothing but food and several thousand people?" she asked.

"Since I signaled we're a slave ship, they shouldn't look too closely," Abdul shrugged. "They'll see all the black people and take us at our word. We'll cram everyone forward so the inspectors see the cramped conditions they expect."

Aamira shook her head. "With as many people as we have on all our ships, the conditions aren't far from what you'd find on a slave ship anyway."

"Except we have much more food, and our people are strong," Abdul replied.

"Won't they think it's strange that an all-black crew and captain are transporting members of their own race for slavery?" Aamira asked.

"Not at all," Abdul answered, wiping rain from his forehead. "There are many black slave traders in these waters; traitors to their kin. They'll sell a child for a single gold piece and not think twice about it. Besides, I already talked to Ryal and Ryland to act as property owners and document holders. Trust me, the inspectors won't look much further than they have to."

As Abdul had said, once the Timbuktu vessel docked, witan inspectors wearing feathered hats and white vests boarded the ship. They talked with the admiral and Ryal before doing a cursory search. They commented about how nice the vessel was, to which Abdul simply replied that Natas and Dameon only accepted the very best. This seemed to make the inspectors nervous, and they quickly marked their ledgers and returned to the docks.

Aamira leaned against the ship's railing and watched the movement on the docks. Hundreds of people milled about, a mixture of slaves and dock workers performing various duties, from loading cargo to mopping spilled ale from a broken cask. A group of two dozen enslaved children marched in a single file line toward a nearby vessel. The children were chained with obsidian around their feet, waists, and neck; chains that jangled as they walked. Aamira knew what these youngsters would face after arriving at whatever plantation had purchased them: work in the fields until they died, or life in a breeding farm as little more than an unpaid prostitute. Anger warmed her skin at the thought of these innocents suffering such a fate.

As the group of children stood around waiting to board their transport, Aamira noticed their backs had protrusions on their shoulder blades that stuck out at least an inch; some even more on several children.

"Adewara," Aamira called. The Educator stepped over from across the deck and looked where she pointed. "Hausan children."

"You're right," Adewara said as he stared down at the scared kids. "Their wings haven't sprouted yet, but they will within the next few years. At that point they'll be amputated before they grow large enough to allow them to fly."

"They look terrified," Aamira said.

"Who can blame them after all that they've had to endure and experience at such a young age." Adewara said.

An idea formed in Aamira's mind. They were masquerading as a slave ship after all, why couldn't they take a few extras in service of the great and terrible Natas?

"Admiral," she shouted, walking toward Abdul through the light rain. "How long until we sail?"

"We're about to pull out now. Why?" he asked.

Aamira stepped toward the gangplank. "We're taking on a few extra passengers. Don't stop anything you're doing, just give me two minutes before you pull up the loading ramp."

Running down to the docks, Aamira weaved through the mass of people and approached a witan sailor holding the end of the children's chains. He wore a sextant around his neck and bit his fingernails absently as she stood before him. Greasy brown hair stuck to his forehead as if it hadn't been washed in a year. His short stature allowed Aamira to tower over him.

"Sailor," she said with the tone of someone official. "I see you have a sextant with you. What is your job under the captain you serve?"

He waved his hand and bit another of his fingernails. "Keep walking, nigger bitch, or I'll have you in chains."

Eye flinching, Aamira manifested a small green knife and pressed it to the man's belly discreetly. She leaned toward his ear and whispered.

"And if you ever speak to me like that again, I'll spill your witan entrails on the dock and watch as they throw your dead body into the surf without even asking what your name was."

The man swallowed and nodded. His eyes shifted back and forth as if looking for rescue.

"Now," Aamira continued, "answer my question."

"I'm the assistant navigator on the *God's Salvation* over there."

God's Salvation. Aamira wanted to kill him right then and there, along with his entire crew. These witans would enslave, rape, and murder, all while thinking their god smiled down on them from their white heaven.

"So, you know the sailing pattern for the next leg of the Nautical Trade."

"Yeah," he nodded.

Aamira let the knife dissipate and stood back up straight. "I am going to pay you 50 gold pieces to take those children onto my ship right here. I know that the going rate of a slave child is one gold piece. There are 24 children here, which means I will be paying you enough to reimburse your captain for the loss, and a hefty payday to you as well. Do you have a problem with that?"

The man smiled with his brownish teeth and shook his head. "No ma'am!"

Aamira led the sailor across the dock and up the gangplank to the Timbuktu vessel. Abdul watched from the deck, smiling.

"Admiral," Aamira said as the children climbed onboard. "We need to pay this man 50 gold for these slave children."

"Do we now?" Abdul grinned.

"Yeah, you do," the sailor sneered, handing the children's chain to the nearest crewmember. "You got a full crew of niggers here? I bet you take longer to do everything than the witan crews," he chuckled.

"He also knows the secret routes for the next leg of our journey," Aamira continued.

Abdul took a deep breath. "Wonderful. Should you chain him up, or should I?"

The sailor's countenance drooped. "What?"

"He should be unconscious first," Aamira said. She turned and slugged the sailor in the jaw as hard as she could, sending him crashing to the deck. He lay there bleeding from the mouth, unmoving.

"Are we ready to sail?" Aamira asked as she wiped blood from her knuckles.

"We are, my empress," Abdul chuckled. "We very much are."

After another week on the currents, the flotilla approached the port of Londone. The size of their fleet had scared off pirates and they sailed unmolested toward land, traveling along the coast of Aban province through the North sea ocean pass.

The Hausan children Aamira had rescued continued to thrive on the ship, running around and playing with the Roman and Rysallian youths. The sailor Aamira had 'conscripted,' named Scraggle, continued to do his duty under threat of torture, though he admitted at one point that the food on this ship was better and there was less yelling. He plotted their course with the admiral and had been surprisingly cooperative. It seemed that beaten animals indeed became less feral when treated with even a modicum of kindness. Aamira had to admit that Scraggle's life prior to joining their voyage had likely been a tragic one, little better than the slaves he would transport. It made her very sad to think about how far humanity as a whole had fallen since Natas decided to make things 'better.'

Aamira dreaded seeing her old home territory of Londone once again. She stood on the ship's prow as crew members pulled on ropes and adjusted the sails. High winds blew from the green lands in the distance, forcing the mariners to shift the riggings in an attempt to keep them on course. The afternoon sun had burned off all the clouds. A deep azure sky stared down on the ocean and its wayfarers.

It had been over 30 years since Aamira had escaped this place with Abioye; a lifetime ago. Yet she knew it had likely changed very little in the decades since the slave riots. Change was not something the residents of Londone, or Lucedale Colony as a whole, were interested in. They had power, so why should anything change?

Aamira thought for a moment about the estate where she grew up and how she had been cared for by Delphine Lalaurie. 'Cared for' was of course a relative term. Delphine had been domineering to the point she had convinced Aamira to treasure her captivity. On the very night of the slave rebellion, Aamira had gone to sleep thinking it wouldn't really happen, and she would get to stay comfortable for the rest of her life without having to sacrifice anything.

What a foolish, stupid child, Aamira thought.

And what of the Lalaurie sisters? They had to be in their late 70's at this point. Were they still alive and just as cantankerous and vile as ever? Still plotting and manipulating each other?

Aamira hoped she would never find out.

Then she remembered Braémah, her nurse and teacher. It had been Braémah that facilitated the riots and performed all of Solomon's orders, not Aamira. It had been Braémah that sacrificed herself so Aamira could escape. Was Braémah still alive, or had she been hanged after the riots as a conspirator?

A tear trickled down her cheek as Aamira thought about the wonderful woman and the care she had given to a young naïve girl. Hopefully she would be proud to see what Aamira had become, and what she had accomplished in trying to free all their people across Aarde.

"Be prepared everyone, we are entering the next pass," Admiral Abdul warned as he walked up beside Aamira. "You know Londone, Empress?"

"I do," she replied.

"This has never been my favorite port," Abdul admitted. "The food is good, but the population is simply…wretched."

"It used to be home for me," Aamira said, staring at the rolling hills approaching from the south.

Abdul pointed at the gap between Londone and the adjacent islands. "We'll have to stop and pass through inspection again at the northern docks. Cannons from the hill forts will be trained on us the entire time. Anything you can tell us that might give us an advantage?"

"It's been 30 years since I was last here, Admiral. I don't even know if the Lalaurie sisters still run the plantations. Everything could have changed as far as I know."

Nodding his head, Abdul turned and shouted orders to the crew to prepare to dock.

Within an hour, the boats started their entry into Londone Pass. The buildings on the shore seemed unchanged in the last 30 years, except newer structures had been constructed to match what was already there. Every edifice had multi-paned windows and a white exterior, with pitched roofs and wooden framing. Everything looked clean, like a marble mausoleum filled with rotting carcasses. Stone forts sat on the hillsides with hidden cannons ready to fire on any perceived threat. As they sailed closer to the docks, Aamira noticed a large number of Trinity soldiers standing at attention, far more than she ever saw when she lived in the area.

"What's happening?" Aamira asked Admiral Abdul as he commented to one of his sailors about the heightened security.

"With the Trinity soldiers?" he asked. "They've increased security, which means several slaves may have escaped over the past few days. Luckily we're just arriving, so I doubt we'll be under the kind of scrutiny the boats that were already here are facing."

Once the ship had docked and dropped the gangplank, witan inspectors in colorful jackets and stockings boarded with manifests and important documents. Ryal and Ryland did most of the talking, using fellow witan Rysallians as guards to make the inspectors feel as if this was just another slave ship. Aamira stood back with a group of passengers wearing the chains they had taken off the Hausan children to make them look more authentically oppressed.

"This is a big ship," one of the inspectors sneered, wiping snot from his pointed nose. "Where does it make berth?"

"N'eropoili," Ryland said without hesitation, his long graying blond hair blowing in the breeze. As a former king himself, he showed no fear in the face of difficult questions. "It was built on Nycea by Lord Damien's personal guard."

Aamira smiled. The mention of Damien, son of Natas, coupled with the size of the vessel, always made the inspectors nervous. Should they question such a claim, or simply take it at face value? They always accepted Ryland's explanation, too afraid to challenge anyone who seemed so confident in their cause.

The inspector swallowed and nodded his head. "Very good. Your documents are in order, and we understand there were no deviations in your course from the prescribed nautical maneuvers. Even so, our matrons are the authority of this port and are personally inspecting all cargo. I understand you have over 100 ships in your fleet?"

"That is correct," Ryland answered.

Again, a terrified look crossed the inspector's face as he glanced at his fellow magistrates.

"Such a force is…unusually large," the pointy-nosed man coughed.

"We are transporting high-value slaves from the Rysallian lands on the other side of the Wall south to Zanstana," Ryland said. "These slaves are to be used as sport for the armies of Lord

Commander Natas. It will be a great honor for the men, women, and children in our armada to die in service to the Lord Commander. Our Lord Natas is particularly interested in children of Sahael. If you have any here in Londone, we will pay handsomely for them."

Again, Aamira smiled. Ryland played his part to perfection. Since rescuing the Hausan youths, Aamira had told him to try and get access to as many enslaved kids as possible for rescue. By the inspector's excited grin, they indeed had some children they would be willing to sell.

"I think we can come to an accord on some high value Sahaelian children to add to your brood," the inspector replied.

"Draw up the paperwork, and we can take them off your hands and be on our way," Ryland said.

Just then, an old woman shouted from the gangplank. It was a voice Aamira recognized even after all these years.

"Who's ship is this? It makes our Londone ships look like fishing boats. It's important! I know it!"

Up the walkway strolled Delphine Lalaurie and her sister Martha. The years had not been kind to either of them. They had never been particularly pretty to begin with, but now age had wrinkled their angry faces like pale prunes. Martha walked with a cane, but Delphine still stood tall and thin despite age's ravaging effects.

Suddenly Aamira's heart beat faster. She could kill these women easily, without a thought, and yet somehow they still had power over her. Memories of Delphine reading to her in the parlor of the manor house about how witans were superior to blacks, and training Aamira to speak only when spoken to, suddenly surfaced in her mind. Did they still search for her after all these years? Had her true importance as a queen of Sahael reached the ears of her old oppressors?

The madams talked with Ryland and Ryal before wandering around the deck, inspecting the crew and slaves. Ryland flirted with the women shamelessly. He stroked his gray beard and laughed with them about how easy it was to oppress black people. Ryland knew how to walk in wealthy witan circles, that was for sure.

"I'm looking for three girls who ran away some years ago, Captain," Delphine Lalaurie said to Ryland, taking hold of his arm as they walked toward the group of people standing around Aamira.

"Would these be slave girls?" Ryland asked with a practiced smile.

"More than that," the old woman said. "It turns out they were more important than we knew. Lord Commander Natas is looking for them as well. They are princesses of Sahael. Apparently they have been causing him problems for the past few decades, in Iceoth and IFF particularly. Have you heard anything on the waters of tall black women with glowing blue, green, or gray eyes?"

Ryland glanced quickly at Aamira as they passed by.

"I have," the Rysallian king admitted.

Delphine stopped. "You have? Where?"

"Word reached me that one of these queens, one with green eyes, took position of the Nibiru Wall last year. From what I understand, she sailed into the west to hunt Enneads. It's one of the reasons we were ordered to sail with such a large fleet. This queen is apparently terrifying and dangerous."

Eyes blinking, Delphine nodded. "She always was something special, Captain. I kept her safe, you know. She never wanted for anything. I would argue with my sisters that my Aamira was the sweetest of the bunch. That Oadira was always causing trouble, and Heziara had her head in the clouds, but my Aamira was sweet and docile. I taught her everything she knows. I don't think she would have left if she hadn't been forced to do it by all those rebelling slave bastards. She was such a joy."

Ryland led the old woman off the ship as she talked about sending search parties to find Aamira in the years after her disappearance. That's how Delphine described it; a 'disappearance,' not an escape, as if Aamira would never have left of her own accord.

And maybe she wouldn't have if Solomon and Braémah hadn't pushed her to it. Maybe she would have stayed at the plantation house and been given to the winner of the Royal Rumble as his breeding prize. Aamira couldn't even remember the man's name, only that he was a servant of Solomon who never would have touched her inappropriately. Even so, Delphine spoke the truth. If Aamira hadn't been forced to flee, she wouldn't have left the plantation. She had lacked the strength of will to set off without forced encouragement, so lost she had become in the comfort of her life.

A sad realization, but a true one, nonetheless.

Once Delphine was off the ship, Aamira took a deep breath. What had happened to this world? Why did people enslave each other? Could Delphine have been something wonderful in another life where slave trading didn't exist? Could she have been a kind protector who didn't keep slaves and have them beaten for not working hard enough?

It didn't matter.

This was the world.

Delphine and her sisters *did* own slaves. They *did* have them beaten and hanged. No amount of personal kindness could wipe away that stain.

Over the next hour, more slave children were brought onto the ship. These children had emerald eyes; every one of them. A continuous obsidian rope was tied around their necks. They walked slowly in a single file line.

Adewara came over to Aamira as she watched the children being escorted onto the vessel by local witan sailors.

"These are children born in the provinces who are being shipped out west to Naharis's realm along with the other children to be killed systematically," he whispered.

"They're Yoruban," Aamira said. "Just like me. Their green eyes give them away."

"Yes," Adewara nodded. "I heard some of the sailors say that once the Yoruban kids get to Naharis's realm, Lord Commander Natas wanted to tie an obsidian stone to the rope around their necks and throw them into the deepest part of the Aeillis Straits and watch as they drown."

Exhaustion seemed to weaken Aamira's knees. How could such evil exist? How could anyone, witan, black, god or monster, be a part of something like this? And yet there were thousands of people right now in Londone who lived in this system and never questioned it.

"I hate this," Aamira said, rubbing her eyes. "It's all so…normal. No one stands up and stops children from being drowned, so long as it's not their children being drowned. How can Ishtar and Obatala sit back and let any of this happen? Why don't they just wipe their hands across the world and destroy all of it?" Why are all these Yoruban children in obsidian chains?"

Adewara placed his hand on Aamira's shoulder. "I understand your anger. Remember, it was me who wanted to cast off the witans of the Rysallian line while you fought for them. We don't understand ourselves, let alone the plans of our creators. As the signs of the times start, the young shall be exposed each time an event is triggered. The Currents, the Quakes, the Tornadoes, and the removal of Deliquesce's seal. They're triggered by the eyes of the children who were born as slaves who'll have their bloodlines exposed. Our being here is no coincidence. It's not luck. It's just as it was supposed to be. And remember also, your actions have meaning. Look at these children; dozens of the Yoruban line who will now be saved because you made a choice. And on top of that, a deposed witan king of the Rysallian line was integral to our survival because he pretended to be an evil captain intent on enslaving blacks. Imagine where we would be right now if I had had my way and Ryland and Ryal were not permitted to come with us. I may be an Educator, but my education is not yet complete."

"The Signs of the times are falling upon us," Aamira said with a smile.

"That's why the Madame and her sisters are looking for you and your cousins even after all these years. Obviously from what I heard from Madame Delphine Lalaurie as she toured the deck with Ryland, everyone knows about you now. That is why the Trinity is here trying to systematically search for you to prevent the gathering from happening."

"These events happening around Aarde are causing these children, whose eyes were once brown, to shine green as if in defiance of Natas," Aamira said.

"Exactly. Natas would rather they be drowned than even be slaves." Adewara turned and looked directly into Aamira's eyes. "Natas is afraid. You have to understand that. He is powerful, yes. He killed the great kings of Sahael, including your own father, yes. But he knows that the end victory is growing farther from his grasp, not closer. I have no doubt, whether in our lifetime or some future generation, Natas will fall, and our posterity will live in peace."

"What're we going to do until then?" Aamira asked.

"We are going to continue the Nautical pattern," Adewara answered. "We can't deviate at this moment. We have more eyes on us now than ever. If we have one mishap, all our human cargo will be blown out of the water. Let's get these children safely onboard and set sail again. Hopefully the other ships in our fleet will make it through safely as well. It will take days for them to make it all through, but we will soon set our eyes on Alkebulan, and one day soon, the city of Sahael."

A cry from across the deck drew Aamira's attention to a group of sailors talking animatedly with Admiral Abdul.

"We should see what's happening," Adewara said.

The two of them walked over to the group, hearing snippets of conversation.

"They were albino!" one of the sailors cried.

"Some of them were being forced into barrels for transport!" another shouted.

"What's going on?" Aamira asked loudly, halting the chatter.

"My Empress," a soldier said with a bow, "some of us went ashore to buy supplies. We saw more children, but these with blue eyes, being herded into barrels for slave transport."

"Orishan children!" Adewara interrupted.

"And on another ship across the dock," another soldier continued, "we saw hundreds of Demirrian Albinos being off-loaded to a large crematorium where they were going to be gassed to death as abominations. The symbol of Natas was painted on the walls of the building. Smokestacks rose from the roof. We need to retrieve those and get them on this ship as soon as possible."

Crematorium? They were simply going to burn the albinos? At that moment Aamira wanted to burn the entire city of Londone and every witan in it.

"We don't have much time," Aamira said.

"We have to save those children." Adewara agreed.

Abdul shook his head. "We can't."

"Why not?" Aamira asked impatiently.

"We are beyond capacity as it is," Abdul stated. "The ship is already dangerously heavy in the water. We can't add hundreds more people. We can't carry enough food to keep everyone alive for the rest of the journey."

Clenching and unclenching her fist, Aamira knew Abdul spoke true. They had already pushed past their limits to get so many people onto the ships with the requisite supplies. To add a couple hundred more people, even if they were only children, would put the entire fleet at risk.

But it didn't matter.

She would not let innocents suffer. If Ishtar and Obatala were truly the gods of creation, they could find a way to feed all these people.

"No," Aamira said, head shaking. "We will save these children and take them with us to Sahael. If they don't make it to the shores of our homeland then none of us will. By Ishtar and Obatala, we will save these children and be blessed for having done so. I have faith. Who is with me?"

A shout rose from the gathered crew and passengers.

Aamira looked at Admiral Abdul. "Will you trust in your Empress?"

"Always," he replied with a bow.

"Then get ready! We're heading to the crematorium and saving everyone we can. Prepare for a fight! No one who stands in our way will be left alive!"

CHAPTER IV
TREACHEROUS PATHS

Londone, Lucedale Colony, Aarde

The sun had set by the time Aamira, her sons and husband, along with a cadre of Rysallian soldiers, were ready to leave the ship. Ryland, Ryal, and Rashida had asked to come as well.

Torches were lit along the docks casting their warm glow on the shops and restaurants of the port. Sailors still loaded crates onto ships, but the majority of work had been completed for the day.

The party left the ship as stealthily as possible, trying to draw little attention to the group's movements. They moved quickly between buildings and empty courtyards, passing a bar where patrons sang loudly and got drunk on Lucedale liquor.

"That last time I saw an Albino was during the Royal Rumble," Aamira whispered to Abioye.

"I've never seen one," Yemí said from behind his mother.

"Are they rare?" Yekú asked.

"These Demirrians are Black Albinos and once numbered in the hundreds of millions," Adewara said.

"Then why haven't we seen any of them out in the open?" Yinká questioned.

"Due to the curse that was placed upon them by Lord Commander Natas after the fall of Sahael," Adewara replied, darting past a lit window and holding to the shadows. "The Children were a part of a curse created by Natas to help wipe out their entire bloodline. It's called the Blight Curse. Natas teaches his followers that the Demirrians are a disease cast upon Aarde to destroy it. Natas made them targets to be hunted by the witans at all times without any repercussions."

"That's terrible," Abioye said. He followed close behind Adewara with Aamira at his side.

For her part, Aamira knew all of this. It was one of the few things she still remembered from Solomon's teachings over thirty years before. He had described in great detail the slaughtering of albinos during one of her education sessions. She had nightmares that night where she saw black albinos burned to death or saw them get their arms and legs chopped off before witan overlords threw what remained to hungry dogs.

The group continued traveling stealthily through the town for another hour, dodging patrols of Trinity soldiers and lovers out for a late-night stroll. As they drew closer to the crematorium, Aamira could smell burning meat and feel ash floating in the air.

"We're close," one of the sailors who had seen the Demirrian children earlier that evening whispered.

"Can we expect any resistance?" Ryal asked.

Rashida shrugged. "I would assume so. They don't leave slaves to their own devices."

Aamira stepped out of an alley into a large industrial courtyard with several brick buildings whose loading doors faced a cobblestone thoroughfare that ran directly to the south docks.

Torches lit the area well enough for her to see a group of ten Trinity soldiers sitting at a table by the loading doors eating their evening meal.

Abioye pointed at a squat building just past where the soldiers sat. He turned to Aamira. "That's a barrack. When I was here as a spy a few days before we met, it's where prisoners were housed before being sent to work in the factories. It looks like the factories have been turned into crematoriums. I would bet our Demirrian kids are in that barrack."

Aamira looked at her four sons. "Boys? It's time for some reconnaissance."

"Yes ma'am," Yemí grinned.

The boys slipped into the dark and didn't return for another 20 minutes. When they did, they shared their findings.

"We saw where they're being kept," Yekú said.

"Father was right," Yinká agreed. "The children are in the barracks. There are the ten guards eating over there, with another 40 patrolling the area. They're Trinity, but obviously not elite soldiers by any means."

"There's more than just children though," Yemí added. "There were at least a hundred albino adults in there as well, along with another hundred Orishan people with blue eyes. We're looking at probably three or four hundred more people."

"Abdul won't like that," Abioye said, shaking his head.

"No one gets left behind," Aamira said. "I've never been the one to have blind faith, but I need to believe in something right now. We need to save these people."

"They look scared," Yinká said. "Like this is going to be their last night in Aarde."

Aamira let out an angry breath. "It won't be. Take out the

guards as silently as you can. We need to get the people back on the ship and sail off before anyone knows what happened. If we're caught, it could put the rest of our fleet in danger from the cannons on the hill forts. Move quietly and deadly. Let's go."

Like shadows, the boys did their work. Aamira had trained them well. Before the soldiers sitting at the table had a chance to cry out, their throats had been cut. Ryal, Ryland and Rashida joined in as well, making quick work of the guards.

"What do we do with the bodies?" Rashida asked. "We can't leave them here. Someone will find them and sound the alarm."

Ryal walked over and opened the loading door. He poked his head in and motioned for Rashida to follow him. "Rashida, my father and I can throw the bodies into the furnace. No one will know what happened to the guards. And there's plenty of blood already in the cobblestones and dirt, so whatever mess we make certainly won't draw attention."

"Smart," Aamira smiled. "You three handle things here. The rest of us will take out the sentries and drag the dead back to be burned."

It took another hour, but by the time the moon rose over Londone's warehouse district, another 40 Trinity soldiers were dead. Aamira had killed seven herself. Only one of them had been able to shout an alarm, but it didn't seem anyone had heard it. Once the area was cleared of enemies, Aamira dispatched her sons to drag the corpses to the furnaces while she, Abioye, and the sailors entered the barracks.

"Leave all your belongings! We have to go now!" Aamira shouted. The room was filled to the brim with people sleeping like dogs in a kennel. Albinos and blue-eyed black children sat up scared and startled. "Get up! Let's go! you're safe now. I am Empress Aamira of the Yoruban Bloodline. We sail for Sahael.

You are welcome to join us, if you hurry behind us as silent as the dead."

The children and adults, while somewhat confused, did as they were told. The group moved quickly and quietly through the alleys, but even so, Abioye was forced to kill six more people on the way back who stumbled upon the crowd. None of them had been soldiers.

Aamira could see the pain on his face as Yemí and Yekú took the victims back to the crematorium to be disposed of.

"It's okay," Aamira told her husband as they approached the dark docks. "Those people would have raised the alarm, and all would have been lost."

"I know," Abioye replied quietly. "The last time I was here, I came as an assassin. I was prepared to kill any witan I needed to. But now, after everything we've been through…everything we've seen, I feel more and more like there's nothing but victims everywhere I look. Everyone seems to be enslaved in some way…even me."

Taking her husband's hand tightly, Aamira led the way back to the ship. She didn't know what to say to him. She had been feeling the same way. Her emotions would pivot from pity to rage every time she saw witan atrocities. Had all the people they killed tonight deserved to die?

Probably not.

They were both victims and perpetrators.

Was she any different?

It took another hour to get everyone onboard the ship. During the process, four more dock workers had to be killed to keep things quiet. Instead of taking their bodies back to the furnaces, Aamira's sons simply tossed them into the ocean where their corpses were washed beneath the docks. They would likely be discovered eventually, but not before the ship had sailed.

Almost the moment the last slaves were onboard, Abdul gave the order, and the ship pulled away from the dock into the dark night. Using the stars and his own experience, Abdul guided them safely into open waters. By the time the sun rose, Londone retreated into the distance.

Aamira sat on the steps to the lower deck as the admiral walked by.

"Do you think our little prison break will cause problems for the rest of the fleet?" she asked him.

"Ten of our ships made it through inspection before we did and are waiting for us on the horizon," Abdul answered. "Another ten were in the south docks and were ordered to sail at first light. Hopefully you did a good enough job of disposing of the guards. There will be confusion for a couple days, I'm sure. It's not often an entire company of soldiers goes missing with a couple hundred slaves, but they were set to be terminated, so who knows. What I do know is that we are sailing slower than planned because of the extra weight, and we will run out of food at least a week before we reach the shores of Sahael, which I remind you, is uninhabitable and lifeless. I trust you, Empress, but I see only difficulty ahead of us."

Standing, Aamira nodded to the admiral. "I appreciate your honesty. You trust me, and I can only trust in Ishtar and Obatala."

"You've found your faith?" he asked.

Aamira shrugged. "It's like I told my crew last night; at this point, all I've got is faith."

Three days later Aamira, Abioye, Adewara, Lanae, and the admiral met in his quarters. They sat at his navigating table eating dried meats. Portions were small, as all food was being rationed to the fullest extent possible. Hunger would soon become a constant on the ship. The room tilted back and forth slightly as the waves rocked them along.

"I need you to understand the magnitude of what's going to happen," Admiral Abdul said candidly as he chewed on his small portion of jerky.

"The Signs of the Times are upon us," Adewara said as he looked everyone in the eyes.

"Time is unfolding right before our eyes," Lanae said.

Admiral Abdul held up his hand. "That's all well and good. I appreciate your belief, but as admiral, I have the reality of our situation to deal with here. We're sailing toward Sahael and the Alkebulan continent, and that is a prophecy fulfilled for those who believe, but we have more pressing issues at hand. I've communicated through hand signals with the rest of our fleet. It's taken three days for word to return. Two of our ships were held in port at Londone. I can't say what's happened, but I'm willing to bet they've been captured because of what happened at the crematorium. We may have saved four hundred people, but we likely lost two thousand because of this."

Sweat began collecting on Aamira's upper lip.

"Beyond that," Abdul continued, "our ships had to move so quickly through port that they were not able to get all the supplies they needed either. We're looking at our entire fleet, one hundred thousand people, possibly starving to death. If you've ever been on a ship where people are hungry, you know the danger grows exponentially every day. I've seen it. Starving people are not rational, nor do they follow orders. I hate to be the bearer of dark news, but I am a speaker of truth, especially on the waters of a perilous ocean."

The group sat silent for a moment.

Adewara spoke first. "I know the choice to save the Demirrian and Orishan remnants from Lucedale was a risk and has added to our liabilities, but it was necessary. Empress Adesola made the right choice."

"Can you elaborate on that please to clear up any confusion?" Admiral Abdul asked, a hint of sarcasm to his words.

"The Signs and the Times are two different events that will happen simultaneously," Lanae explained. "One cannot happen without the other. When empress Aamira activated the quakes thirty years ago, it set in motion protections that allowed slaves to escape and find refuge. The quakes have continued however, and those protections have now ended. Death covers the lands. Even so, the gathering is taking place right before our eyes. The four bloodlines are the key to returning to Sahael, through the four chosen bloodlines."

"You're referring to the gathering?" Abioye asked.

"No, not a gathering, but a prelude to the gathering," Adewara replied. "A prelude that will create a spark that will then ignite a gathering never before seen in Aarde. Once the gathering has been ignited, the Black Messiah will descend on Aarde to redeem the Blacks of Sahael, Alkebulan, and the entire world."

Admiral Abdul rubbed his forehead. "I understand the need of Educators to always spout prophecies and such, but you're talking about a gathering at some point in the future. I'm talking about starvation right now. I mean, we have hundreds of children onboard who have no parents; no one to take care of them."

"The families on the ship are caring for the orphans,"

Aamira interrupted.

"And the children are incredibly important to our mission," Adewara added, finger extended like a proper professor. "Without the children from the four bloodlines, there can be no Sahael. Us rescuing them, even finding them in the first place, should prove itself a miracle in and of itself. Do you realize that on this ship alone we have representatives of every bloodline needed to redeem Alkebulan? Without them, we would be sailing toward our deaths. If there is no Sahael then there can be no Alkebulan. If there's no Alkebulan, there can be no Aarde, and If there is no Aarde then all that exists is darkness, anguish, and eternal death."

"I hate to repeat myself, but none of this solves the problem our vessels are facing when it comes to being overcrowded," Abdul stated.

"We will survive, Admiral," Adewara said, standing from his seat and leaning forward against the table. "Some of these children were going to be thrown to the bottom of the Sea of Triennium, killed in gas chambers, or burned alive. We rescued them. We now have all the representatives needed for the prophecies to be fulfilled. I understand this is a matter of faith, but if you can't see how miraculous this all is, then my words will have no meaning anyway. Do you know how the signs are triggered?"

"I've never really thought about it," Abdul admitted, sitting back in his chair as if resigned to a lecture.

Adewara smiled. "When Empress Aamira's cousin Oadira triggered the changing of the currents, she reversed the flow, forcing the waters to move back toward Nier's realm. As the currents were pushed back, the magic from Nier's Realm helped restore Life magic to Aarde. That Life magic not only restored and returned life to Aarde's waters, Orishan magic was unleashed all over Aarde, revealing the eyes of the children of the four ancient bloodlines of Sahael. That is why those children were marked for death. Magic no longer hid their true natures as the next generation of Sahaelians."

"Getting these children back to Sahael will play a pivotal role in how Aarde is going to be shaped," Lanae said, now also standing beside her father. "These children are essential to the growth and prosperity of Sahael. Without them the foundation of Sahael would cease to exist."

"The Lifeblood of any nation is the children," Adewara said with a nod of his head. "They are the future and the hope that we all will look to, to make things right. Natas will do all that is within his power to hunt these children to disrupt the order of balance."

Admiral Abdul stared at Adewara emotionlessly. He blinked several times and took a deep breath. "I understand the children are important, but so is food. How does all of this help us, and the other 99 ships following in our wake, from starving to death within a week. We won't reach Alkebulan within that time. We're now entering the waters of the lower middle passage, which means we're going to face storms and headwinds. All I'm asking is for something concrete; something I can pass along to my captains and all the civilians that will calm their hearts as food runs out."

"Tell us more about the middle passage, Admiral," Aamira said.

"The Lower passage is where slaves were exchanged. It's also a place where witans dumped slaves to sever the bloodlines of Sahael. The witans sailed up the lower passage waters with difficulty, moving their large ships through the treacherous waters. The trip was more bearable due to the currents, and the waters that helped them move up and down and through the dead water pass. We're looking at whirlpools around the Njal Island and who knows what else. There is a reason the waters around Alkebulan are said to be cursed since the fall of Sahael."

"Admiral," Aamira said, touching Abdul's hand. "We were meant to be here right now with the people we have onboard. I have always struggled to lead with faith. I've had times of anger, fear, apathy, but rarely faith. After the trials my family went through to gain this heart…" Aamira pulled on a chain around her neck and revealed the green gemstone hanging there. "…Inkalamu's Heart from Nisine's Monument, I began to understand that my choices are still mine, but they are playing out on a bigger stage than I know. I now fully believe we were meant to find these children, which means we will all survive to set foot on the Alkebulan continent and breathe free air again. You said more than once that you trusted me. If that is true, trust me now."

"I do," Admiral Abdul said after a deep breath.

"Then sail toward Alkebulan, Admiral. Trust me when I say that miracles will manifest along the way."

Within two days, Aamira's promise of miracles was fulfilled. A storm rose, swallowing the fleet. Waves crashed high enough to splash over the sides of the ships, depositing fish that flopped on the deck. Thousands of fish were washed onboard, and Abdul confirmed that the same thing had happened on the other vessels as well.

No one went hungry.

Other dangers persisted, however.

"Pull in the mainsail!" Abdul shouted as rain fell in buckets on the ship. Lightning had struck the mast and caught fire before being doused by the deluge. Aamira, Abioye, and the boys ran alongside sailors desperately attempting to keep the vessel from falling apart. Soaking wet and tired, Aamira yanked on a rope to help keep the sails from unfurling and ripping from the riggings. Her feet slipped on the wet deck, but she held firm.

"Admiral! A whirlpool!" one sailor shouted from the crow's nest.

"Where?" Abdul called back.

"Starboard!"

The ship suddenly lurched to the right, forcing Aamira to plant her feet even more firmly to keep from losing hold of the rope. Wind blew furious though, lifting Aamira into the air.

"Mother!" Yemí cried.

Tilting even further as it was pulled into the whirlpool, the ship's wooden planks screeched against the strain. Aamira, still flapping over the side holding tight to the rope, looked down into a swirling abyss of angry water. Lightning crashed all around.

"Turn the wheel!" Admiral Abdul ordered. "Turn the wheel! Turn the wheel!"

The ship pulled straighter and skirted the vortex's edge. Aamira swung back down to the deck, landing on the wet wood.

"Are you alright?" Abioye asked as he ran up to her.

"I'm fine. I just got a little closer to a whirlpool than I ever wanted to be."

The next few weeks offered similar experiences on an hourly basis. Still, Admiral Abdul did his best to avoid the waterspouts and sinking currents. A constant brigade of bucketers bailed water from the lower decks to keep the ship from drafting any deeper. Miserable conditions persisted, but the crew and passengers worked side-by-side to make sure they stayed afloat.

By the time the storm passed and the sun rose on a cloudless morning, everyone was exhausted, both emotionally and physically.

Aamira walked along the deck, breathing the calm air. She used a knife to cut open a fish and ate the meat raw. Under normal circumstances the combination of uncooked fish and the sway of the sea would have been nauseating, but after so much sailing and hunger, she didn't care so long as she felt full.

"Empress!" Admiral Abdul shouted from the upper deck. He walked down the steps toward her, footfalls heavy and tired.

"Admiral Abdul," Aamira nodded. She tossed the remains of her fish overboard. "It looks like the worst is over."

"I doubt that," the admiral said, leaning over the side, shoulders slumped.

"How long has it been since you've slept?" Aamira asked.

"I got a couple hours yesterday midday," he smiled. "I'll rest when I can. For now, we have a problem. A number of problems, actually."

"What is it?"

"The storm has pushed us farther south than anticipated. I had hoped to sail south and then west toward the Kossi region of Alkebulan. From our bearings this morning though, it looks like we are much farther off-course than anticipated. I would assume that Luongo Province is about 200 miles to the west, and we're coming up on the Sentinel Islands."

"Well, that's good," Aamira said as the wind caught her long braids. "The Sentinel Islands are at the entryway to Sahael's Middle Passageway that leads ships directly to the city. We're what, less than 100 miles from Alkebulan shores?"

"Yes," Abdul nodded. "But the waters around the Sentinel

Islands are known to be incredibly treacherous. There are hidden sholes and rogue waves that can broadside ships and destroy them. If the old tales are to be believed, we won't make it to shore. On top of that, we only have sight on three of our fellow fleet members."

Aamira's chest contracted slightly. "Only three? Out of 100? How is that possible?"

"The storm ravaged us," Abdul confirmed. "We're heavily damaged, our riggings are in disarray and the sails are torn. I can't say if the ships were lost or simply blown off-course. We're not where we planned to be, so it's a good bet the others aren't either. Right now, the currents are pulling us toward the islands in the distance, and we have very little means to escape. No matter what, we're sailing into uncharted waters that have a foreboding history."

Aamira looked over the ocean, seeing dark specks of land on the horizon.

"How long until we arrive at the islands?" she asked.

"At this speed? Tonight sometime. Maybe sooner. Using my spyglass, I was able to see rough seas ahead. And I mean very rough. It looks as if there are whitecaps as tall as this ship, which means the currents are smashing against shallow rocks and kicking up huge waves. If I were a betting man, I'd say we have high odds of running aground and being capsized. "

Here they were, so close to their destination and yet facing yet another obstacle. Aamira thought about the lost ships, praying they survived the storm. If they had sunk, she would have led tens of thousands of people to their deaths. The weight of the possibility devoured what strength she had left.

Still, alive or not, she couldn't worry about the rest of the fleet. Her family, and the children on this boat, still had a mission to accomplish.

"Very well, Admiral," Aamira said. "Alert everyone onboard that there is a possibility of needing to abandon ship at some point, so for them to prepare. I want every child accounted for and shepherded by an adult. If we're forced to abandon ship, those kids need to be able to make it to shore safely. Tell Ryland, Ryal, and Rashida to take the lead with the Romans and Rysallians onboard. My sons are to be put in charge of the families. Have Adewara and Lanae gather supplies that can be taken with us in case the ship sinks. My husband and I will lead the evacuation from the lower decks, if such a thing becomes necessary."

"Yes, my empress," Abdul bowed.

He left immediately.

The next few hours were filled with activity as passengers and crew broke into groups and took responsibility for the children. The dark shapes on the horizon grew closer and closer, and as they did so, the waves became more punishing. By evening, the ship was being tossed up and down like a child's toy in a bathtub.

"Admiral! Sholes ahead!" cried the sailor in the crow's nest. Before Abdul could respond, the ship hit something hard, tossing everyone forward. The sound of shattering wood conflicted with the pounding of surf. The mast splintered suddenly and crashed into the deck, crushing two sailors.

"Hold fast!" Admiral Adbul yelled.

But it was too late.

The ship careened to the left and began to tip as a wave pummeled the port side mercilessly.

"Abandon ship!" Abdul ordered. "Swim toward the islands!"

Everyone on deck leaped over the side frantically. Aamira and Abioye ushered families from the lower decks as quickly as they could. The ship would toss to the right and then back again to the left, each time with greater force. People tripped and slid along the wet wood. The ship began to sink toward the prow.

"Jump! Jump! Jump!" Abioye cried.

Within moments, the front of the ship shattered. A wave crashed against the port side, and what remained of the vessel tipped into the water.

Aamira jumped at the last second. Cold water surrounded her. Currents twisted her about. She held her breath, trying to swim to the surface. When air finally filled her lungs again, she found herself being tossed like a piece of driftwood in a waterfall. All around her people scrambled to swim in the turbulence. A child cried out and sank below the surface, only for a witan Rysallian to emerge holding the little black girl tightly in his arms.

"Toward the island!" Aamira yelled.

Lucky for the swimmers, the waves crashed toward land, pulling them along. By nightfall, Aamira lay in the sand, coughing and helping the tired people stumble from the surf. The island itself was covered in cactus and juniper trees; an arid spot of desert vegetation.

After an hour of pulling people from the ocean, Aamira's sons and husband appeared from down the beach, wet and tired. She rushed up and hugged each of them, kissing Abioye.

"I've been looking for you," she smiled.

"I knew you'd make it to land safe," Abioye grinned. "We just wanted to make sure everyone made it before it became too dark to see."

"It's going to be a miserable night, Mother," Yekú said. "Not much survived the ship. I know a few people brought bags with blankets, but everything is wet, and we have no food."

The stars began appearing overhead.

"We'll need to wait till morning to check our losses," Aamira said. "Go up and down the beach telling everyone to stay together as family units. Once the sun rises, we'll make plans. And if you find Admiral Abdul, tell him we're alright."

That night, Aamira and Abioye snuggled close for warmth as the sand pulled heat from their bodies. No one slept well, and by sunrise, Aamira looked out on over three thousand people clustered along the shore. Other islands sat in the water within a mile of where they stood, looking as dry and barren as their current surroundings.

Yinká ran up the beach, waving in the pale light. "Mother! Father! I found Admiral Abdul. He's okay and is making his way here. Adewara and Lanae are with him. They were able to salvage some of the barrels filled with dried fruits from the currents. Everyone should be able to eat something."

After meeting with the Admiral and taking a headcount, it seemed as if most of the passengers and crew had made it to shore.

"We lost a handful of people to the waves," Admiral Abdul said as they stood next to a collection of boulders overlooking the ocean, "but we got lucky, it seems."

"Blessed," Lanae corrected.

"Father and I were able to grab a few Hausan children struggling in the water," Yomí informed. "Even that sailor you kidnapped, Scraggle, swam back and saved a couple of kids, which surprised me. Maybe he's not such a horrible guy after all. But the real surprise was the Orishans. They swam like fish. It was incredible. They were the first to reach land and keep going back to the water as if it were life itself. Even the Orishan children were strong enough in the currents to rescue adults that were floundering."

Adewara stepped forward. "The Orishan element is water, much like your Yoruban element is earth. Arriving on these islands was no accident. It was providence. We need to search the island. Each of the six Sentinel Islands have Nairohenge gates on them. This is where the six sacred bloodlines would meet with their people. The Sentinels were to be the last line of defense for Sahael to combat any enemies that wanted to destroy the ancient bloodlines. When Sahael was destroyed, the Nairohenge gates retracted into the ground, preventing anyone from having the ability to travel to Sahael, Alkebulan, and the four realms. The Sentinelese were to share the responsibility of protection to the chosen bloodlines, but when Sahael fell, they were left stranded on their home island, neutralizing them entirely."

"So, where are they?" Abioye asked. "I haven't seen any other people beyond the refugees from the ship."

"I'm not sure," Adewara admitted. "Before first light I explored a bit and found a road leading inland, along with a cluster of adobe buildings. It was all in disrepair however, which makes me believe either the habitants were killed by Nata's forces when Sahael was destroyed half a century ago, or the continent becoming uninhabitable somehow effected the islands here as well."

"You mentioned Nairohenge Gates," Aamira said. "Could we find and activate them?"

Shaking his head, Adewara rubbed his graying beard in thought. "No. We don't have any navigators with us. But, we do have representatives of all the bloodlines. According to prophecy, each of the six islands must be populated by members of that bloodline. The Sentinel Islands will then, through the seismic powers of the Yoruban bloodline, be reunited into a single island. I thought this would happen sometime after the redemption of Sahael, but the fact that we arrived here with representatives of each bloodline, I feel now is the moment."

Tapping her finger against the boulder, Aamira tried to picture the six islands being pulled together by seismic forces. She could shake the ground when needed, but moving landmasses was on a completely different level.

"These islands are the ancestral lands of the sacred bloodlines," Lanae said. "That's why each person will be drawn to their island. Each of the six islands has inactive gates. We need the different representatives of the bloodlines to go to the islands that call to them. From there, we need one of the sacred tribes to send one person each to the center of Sentinel Island."

"What purpose will that serve?" Aamira asked.

"At the center of each island, there is an anchor that needs to be released," Adewara answered. "Once released, the anchors will allow each island to amplify the Yoruban quaking arte and be drawn together."

"Tell us what to do," Yemí said.

"When the blood of the six sacred bloodlines is poured in the six slots, the six anchors will be released. Once the anchors are released, the six islands will pull inward and join as one, activating all fifteen Nairohenge Gates," Adewara said.

"How much blood are we talking about here?" Abioye asked.

"The people are weak," Aamira agreed. "We have limited food. It will take days to get people to each island. And we don't have a ship anymore either."

Adewara leaned against the boulder and looked out at the ocean. "The Orishans. They are the key to our survival here. They can swim and catch fish easily, feeding the approximately 3,500 people here with us. We assign leaders to each bloodline group and head to the islands tomorrow. On the third day, we perform the ritual here on the primary isle."

"Who will lead?" Yinká asked, chest suddenly stretching as if filled with power.

"You and your brothers," Adewara confirmed.

Cocking her head toward Adewara, Aamira's brow creased. "That's not your decision to make, Educator."

"Aamira…" Abioye whispered in an attempt to calm the moment.

Adewara stood firm. "Members of the Royal Family will need to be on each island, using their terrakenesis in conjunction with each other. There will be altars in the center of the islands where anchors will need to be pulled as the ground shakes. Your abilities will be the catalyst. Plus, you and your sons are leaders of Sahael as much as your cousins are. The people will listen to them."

"And what happens after the islands are unified?" Aamira asked, teeth pressed together.

"The gates will extend from the ground once more."

"And we can then use them to travel freely?"

"Unfortunately, that won't happen," Adewara said. "The gates won't be operational until the people of the sacred bloodlines all go to their respective cities and acquire Navigators."

"I don't understand," Aamira said.

"The Orishan children will be sent to Sahaedron, the Yoruban children to Sahaeland, and the Hausan children Sahaerion, and the Demirrian children to Sahaedeath," Adewara stated.

"There are no adults to escort the children to Sahaeland and the other cities," Abioye pointed out. "They'll have to stay here along with the others until Sahael is safe to enter."

"Once that is accomplished," Adewara began, "the three Princes, Yekú, Yomí, and Yemí, will lead the children to their cities. King Yinká will lead the Yorubans; Ryal and Rashida, the united Rysallians and Romans. If on your journey you encounter ships from our fleet, divide them up into these same groups and lead them to the cities. Once the Nairohenge gates are operational once again with Navigators and Medjay gate guardians, everyone will be reunited."

"Your sons are required to make a sacrifice for the betterment of Sahael," Lanae said. "It's the only way to get your Kingdom in order and return to Khartoum Palace."

Sand pressed against Aamira's toes as her feet muscles became tense. She wanted to run and kick and scream. Could she not enjoy a moment's rest with her family? Could she not live a moment without prophecy and responsibility? Could her sons not live their lives on their own terms?

"Mother," Yemí said, touching her shoulder. "We're all grown up. Even Yinká."

"Damn right," Yinká grinned.

"Shut up," Yemí smiled. "We're here to serve as you and Father have served. We grew up safe in a realm of frozen time. You trained us. We've fought and killed. Let us protect now. Let us help our people."

Aamira looked into her son's eyes and saw him as the powerful man he was. These boys had already suffered so much. The three oldest were in their thirties and yet had never had the chance to marry or start their lives. Now they were being asked to sacrifice again.

But she knew they were ready for it.

"Okay," she nodded. "You boys each lead one of the peoples to their island. In four days, we'll perform the ritual here and the islands will be unified…" She looked at Adewara. "In theory. As much as I hate to admit it, Adewara has been right. Our faith brought us here alive. We'll continue to travel in faith. Once the islands are united, each group will be on its own to make their way to the cities. I've looked at the maps. This will take weeks, maybe months."

"And Sahael is still uninhabitable, right?" Yinká asked.

"As far as we know," Aboye answered.

"And we don't have any boats," Yekú added.

Again, Aamira looked at the waves crashing nearby. They had come this far without knowing what the next day would bring. But now they were stranded with no resources and a hundred miles of ocean between them and Alkebulan. If she thought logically, only starvation and death seemed like realistic possibilities.

Thinking logically wouldn't solve their problems though.

In that moment, a feeling of peace seemed to fill Aamira's chest. She breathed deeply through her nose, smelling the salt in the air and feeling the warm breeze against her skin.

They would be alright.

"I don't have any answers," she said, turning back to face the group. "I don't know how we'll survive once we arrive in Sahael. I don't know how we'll even get to Sahael. But I know we will. I can't explain it, I just know. You boys will lead the people. Once the islands are united, search for any boats or crafts you can find. These islands were inhabited once, which means we have resources. Make your way to the mainland and find the cities. The rest of us, me, your father, Adewara, Lanae, and the Admiral, will make our way to the Middle Straight. If the air is unbreathable, I'm sure a way will be provided for us to survive. I have faith. I give that faith to all of you as well."

The boys hugged their mother, crying with smiles on their

faces. With so much unknown, they gave themselves to the gods for protection.

As they broke their embrace, Aamira looked at the crowds standing on the beach expectantly. "Spread the word, boys. The Orishans need to start bringing in fish and the people need to prepare to make it to the adjacent islands at dawn tomorrow. On the third day after that, we shake Aarde and bring these lands together before making our final journey…home."

The four days passed quickly.

Aamira took that time to explore the main Sentinel Island on which they had been shipwrecked. A decaying city acted as the center, with a large courtyard where the circularly placed Nairohenge Gate stones had pulled into the ground five decades before. The buildings were made of stone and concrete, appropriate for the desert landscape. No signs of battle scarred the city, making Aamira think that either the people simply abandoned the islands once Sahael fell, or the climate changes that occurred immediately afterward made life here impossible.

At the direct center of the island, ringed by the sunken stones of the Nairohenge Gate, stood an altar of fine marble. Six sinks were carved into the surface, with a round anchor-like pulley of iron sticking out of the top, adorned with the sacred Ankh symbol.

Aamira looked at Adewara, who stood with three little girls, one from the Orishan line, one from the Hausan, and one from the Demirrian. Rashida stood behind him with Ryal. She had chosen to represent the Roman, Ryal the Rysallian, and of course

Aamira would represent the Yoruban. Lanae, Abioye, and Admiral Abdul stood back, watching the scene unfold.

Everyone approached the six anchor altar slots.

"You all need to make your way to the center," Adewara said, ushering the girls forward. They seemed scared, but strong.

"The women have been leading this change," Aamira grinned to the girls. "You are part of a long line of strong women." She looked at Ryal and nodded. "But it's time for everyone to start playing an active role in helping us get to Sahael."

"All of you need to give equal amounts of blood to fill the grails and allow your blood to fill the six slots," Adewara said.

Starting with the little girls, Adewara cut the inside forearm muscles of everyone, ensuring that he would have enough blood. The girls cried quietly as blood dripped down their arms and into the sinks.

"Hold your arms over the cup until it fills up with blood of the innocent," Adewara said. He turned to Rashida and Ryal, cutting them in the same way. Finally, Aamira stepped forward. The blade sliced painlessly through her flesh. Warm blood dripped from her arm onto the altar.

"After the sinks are filled, each grail will emanate a sapphire, emerald, Hematite, and turquoise color," Adewara said.

Moments later, the sinks were filled and Aamira grabbed cloth to wrap up the girl's arms. Rashida and Ryal helped before tending to their own cuts. As they wrapped their arms, the altar sinks began to glow with color, just as Adewara had said they would.

"Now is the time." Adewara motioned for Aamira to touch the anchor protruding from the altar. She grabbed it with both hands, immediately feeling the vibrations of the ground beneath their feet.

"How do we know our sons have found the anchors on their islands?" she asked.

"We don't," Adewara replied. "We simply have faith."

Closing her eyes, Aamira channeled her power into the anchor like a tuning fork. Each granule of sand called out to her. She felt pebbles and rocks a hundred feet beneath the surface. Aarde shook suddenly with violent force.

A shockwave shot from the altar. With her eyes still closed, Aamira heard the cries of the girls and the worried grunts of Abioye. Buildings collapsed in the city around her, but she held firm and channeled her power back into Aarde.

The ground shook for an hour. Aamira never once opened her eyes, choosing instead to feel the power of the planet coursing through her fingers.

Eventually, the quake subsided. Aamira fell to the ground, completely exhausted. Abioye rushed over and held her in his arms.

"She needs water!" he shouted. "Her skin is hot to the touch! She's burning up."

"I'm…okay," she replied, opening her eyes. Her husband's worried face stared down at her. "I'm okay. It was…glorious. I could feel our sons. Each of them found the anchors. We were connected. The islands…are united. I can feel it in the ground even now. Aarde…whispers to me."

Abioye grabbed the thin gold chain around Aamira's neck and pulled out Inkalamu's Heart. The green crystal glowed faintly.

"As the ground shook," Abioye said, "the Heart glowed like green fire. At one point it looked like the fire consumed you completely. It blazed for a half hour during the quake. It's as if you activated Inkalamu's Heart with your actions."

After spending some time drinking water and regaining her strength, Aamira stood and looked around. Most of the city was in ruins, but the Nairohenge Gates, with their collection of tall square-columned stones, stood bright and tall in the sunshine.

"The gates are still not operational," Adewara said. "Until we can return to Sahael, they cannot be fully activated. Still, they are above ground. Once they are activated, the Romans can return to their homeland, as can all the free peoples. It will be a joyful time."

As Adewara spoke, the stones of the gate suddenly began to glow.

"What's happening?" Abioye asked.

"I don't know!" Adewara answered.

Wind blew and lightning crackled form the gate. A portal of greenish-blue light appeared. The form of a man took shape, until two people stepped from the portal. One was older, six-feet nine-inches tall, with very dark skin, and a metal signet on his forehead bearing the sigil of the Sentinel Islands. He had a nose ring, ivory teeth, and wore a black cloak. The other man, Aamira recognized immediately.

"Yinká!" she cried, rushing forward to hug her son. "What is going on? How did you get here?"

Yinká laughed. "We met Segodi and the remnants of the people of Sentinel on our island when we arrived on shore two days ago. He helped us find the anchor altar and accessed the gate."

The old man, Segodi, stepped forward. "Your son has told me much about you, Empress Adesola, Queen of Sahael. Since my youth I have dreamed of a time when the continent of Alkebulan would be redeemed, and I would once again see the beauty of our land restored."

Adewara stared at the portal, mouth open. "You know how to access the gates?"

"I do," Segodi replied in his quivery voice. "Or at least, Katartina does. We have a Navigator among my people. She is as old as I am, but she still remembers how to make it work. Unfortunately, she could only create an access link with six of the fifteen gates on the Sentinel Islands and none on the continent of Alkebulan."

"How many people survive on your island?" Lanae asked the old man.

"Only around 700. These islands used to be home to tens of thousands before the Narsan destroyed Sahael. Survival has been difficult, but the southernmost island, Sentinel Sul, still has fresh water and orchards. From what your son has told me, we can now walk between the islands, which seems impossible to me."

"It's possible," Yinká grinned. "My mother makes all kinds of things possible."

"Don't give me undue credit," Aamira said. "I'm making things up as I go along, and Ishtar is picking up the slack."

"Well said, my liege," Segodi bowed. "I understand you are planning to go to the mainland. Currents have shifted over the past month. Clean waters have flowed from Alkebulan for the first time since the Great Fall. Fish have been more abundant than in many decades."

Aamira looked at Adewara. "Clean waters?"

A tear formed in the Educator's eye. "If the waters are clean, that means someone has restored the lifeblood of Sahael! It's the only explanation."

Muscles relaxing, Aamira remembered when they arrived at Timbuktu. Oadira had already been there, activating the Orishan symbols. Adewara had said his wife, Lyshyla, had been with her as well.

"Oadira," Aamira whispered. "She did it. It had to be her."

"We don't know for sure this means life has returned to Alkebulan," Lanae warned. "We must still proceed with caution."

"Then we need to get going," Adewara clapped. "We are close, but only the Empress can direct us now."

"How? I don't know where to go," Aamira said.

"You will know in time," Adewara assured.

Segodi raised his withered hand. "I will transport you across the middle passage to the Yoruba forest," he said. " We have fishing boats that can brave the open waters to Alkebulan. There we can confirm if the lands have been healed. Follow me. Everyone else will be safe until we confirm Sahael is safe to enter."

Without warning, Aamira began to cry.

She was finally on the cusp of reaching Sahael.

Before they set sail for the mainland, Aamira was able to see her sons again. The activated gates made traveling across the new landmass quick and easy. Segodi's Sentinel people lived simply, in thatched homes of thick dried grass that had survived the devastating quake. The royal family ate dinner with them and slept well, but by morning, time had come to set off. The boys decided to remain with the bloodlines they had traveled with, promising to lead them to their cities on Alkebulan. Only young Yinká would be coming with them to Sahael. Admiral Abdul, impressed with the ship-building prowess of the Sentinelese people, decided to stay back and help them build larger vessels that could take the people to shore more easily.

So it was on the fifth day from their arrival on the Sentinel Islands that Aamira, Abioye, Adewara, Lanae, and Yinká, led by Segodi and Abrobi, one of his sons, set off in a large fishing boat toward the shores of Alkebulan.

Rough waters greeted the boat, tossing them about much more violently than the large Timbuktu vessel they had sailed in prior. Still, the fishing vessel had a small lower deck where Aamira and the crew could dry off and seek shade from the sun. They fished as they traveled and cooked the meat on stones that could be quickly heated with coals in a manner Aamira had never seen before. Even Adewara was impressed by the ingenious invention.

On the third day at sea, Segodi spotted land in the distance. Aamira couldn't see it at first, but a few hours later, a thin green line appeared on the horizon to the east.

"Alkebulan and the Middle Passage," Segodi said. "As you can see, the waters are clear and clean. This used to be as far as we would sail because the ocean became so poisoned. Not since my younger days have I sailed toward Sahael. I am blessed."

"What can we expect once we enter the Middle Passage?" Abioye asked as he tossed a coil of rope to Abrobi.

"Death," Segodi replied.

"What do you mean?" Aamira asked. "You just said the waters were clean. Why would we find death in a land healed by my cousin Oadira?"

"Partly healed," Adewara corrected. "Remember, you still have missions to perform in the healing as well. Plus, we don't know to what extent Sahael, and the surrounding lands have been redeemed. Is it just the water? We have no idea. We must measure our expectations."

"But why would we find death?" Yinká questioned.

Segodi stood on the prow of the wooden boat and stared at the land on the horizon.

"As bodies wash up on the sentinel shores," he said, "we intentionally place the skeleton or bodies in a boat and send them right back into the middle passage waters once again,"

"Why? Aamira asked.

"We made an agreement centuries ago with Sahael to protect the people in life and death. Solomon, the protector of Aarde, also instructed us to preserve the skeletons, and they would one day help bring back life to Sahael. We will likely encounter these skeletons and bodies as we enter the middle passage."

Yinká tied a knot in one of the lines running up to their single sail. "But why would the bodies be preserved? They should sink and decay pretty fast, right?"

"Sacred lands are sacred for a reason," Segodi answered.

"I know personally that many of the Yoruban slaves were thrown overboard after the sacking of Sahael by an order handed down by Lord Commander Natas," Adewara said. "He was in a fit of rage apparently after not securing the four bracelets and the princesses who wore them. Natas had those with green eyes thrown overboard one by one, and the rest were sent to the provinces."

Looking down at the water passing by the hull, Aamira imagined dead faces looking up at her; the faces of her kin.

As Segodi had implied, the next day they sailed up the middle passage, past the open Orichalcum gate that once guarded the interior lands. The passage felt like a river as they entered, though the banks moved quickly apart until they could only see one shoreline. For now, they followed that coast until once again the land would come back together on the shores of Sahael itself. The forest on the left looked withered and dry, but alive. The air was breathable.

"Change has occurred here," Adewara said as he watched the shore move past them. He turned to Aamira. "One of your cousins, whether Oadira or another, has indeed broken the curse of the land. Still, as you can see by the state of things, true redemption has not yet come to pass, at least for this section of Alkebulan."

"Look!" Yinká shouted, pointing at the water.

Dead bodies floated on the surface, some little more than skeletons, others bloated and decaying. A stench rose from the water. Most of the bodies had a glowing green symbol on their foreheads that Aamira had never seen before.

"What are those markings on their heads?" Abioye asked.

Suddenly, Aamira and Yinká's eyes began to glow with emerald light. Inkalamu's Heart lit up with Zambian fire around Aamira's neck as well.

"What's happening?" Abrobi asked, stepping back with shock on his face. He drew a symbol on his chest with his finger, as if warding off evil.

The necklace tugged on Aamira's neck, as if wanting to dive into the water. It pulled and pulled again. In her mind she heard voices suddenly, as if the dead were speaking from some great distance.

Let us serve, the voices said. *Let us serve even in death.*

"Inkalamu's Heart wants to touch the water," she said as she unclasped the necklace and looked at the flaming jewel.

"What does that mean?" Abioye asked.

Silently, Aamira knelt on the side of the boat and lowered the jewel to the water. As Inkalamu's Heart touched the surface, the green flame, as if sucked into the depths, infected the water itself. The dead bodies with marks on their foreheads started to emanate an emerald color, causing the symbols to turn Zambian. Then, as if dissolving, the skeletons and corpses broke down into an oily substance that infected the inlet, followed the boat as they sailed.

"What is happening?" Yinká asked. "Adewara, do you know what's going on?"

"I don't," he said, head shaking slowly. "But look at the shoreline."

Aamira stood, glancing toward the dry forest. The ground seemed to be soaking up the oil, revitalizing the plants. Leaves that moments before had been dry and sickly, expanded into lush, robust foliage.

"The physical material from the bodies is giving life to the land itself," Abioye gasped.

"Yes," Aamira confirmed as she reclasped the necklace. "The dead wanted to serve the living and heal Sahael. That's why they have been floating here for so long. I think the pollutants that were in the Middle Passage before the healing kept them preserved until now." She looked at Adewara and Lanae. "We're a part of something bigger and more important than I ever knew."

"We are," Adewara smiled.

Unfortunately, Segodi's son didn't see it that way. As soon as they drew close to shore, he demanded they drop off their passengers and return home to avoid any curses. Segodi tried to reason with the man, but Abrobi was adamantly superstitious.

"It's fine," Aamira told the old man. "We can make it from here. I have a feeling we'll find out path."

"This is where I leave you then, Empress. My faith travels with you!" Segodi said as they stepped off the boat. The fishing vessel turned around and headed back toward the ocean.

Aamira stood there for a moment in the wet soil of Alkebulan. Mud squished between her toes. She relished the cool feeling.

She had made it to her homeland.

After so many years of sacrifice, prophecy and pain, Aamira, daughter of Enqui and Arishkegal, stood on the borders of Sahael, breathing the air of her ancestors.

Abioye bent over and placed his hands in the water. "These people died so we could be here today with the ability to restore what should've been restored centuries ago. Our people will be united and never fracture because of pride again.

"Yes, Father," Yinká said.

"It's time to move on," Adewara said, cutting off any further conversation. "We need to make our way to Sahael. We still don't know what we'll find there. Aamira just proved that death is still holding strong to the continent, waiting for us to heal it. Let's enter the Black Forest and make our way north."

The group, led by Aamira, left the banks of the passage and plunged into the dense forest. What mysteries awaited them, they could only guess.

CHAPTER V
EMERALD SAHAEL

Alkebulan, Yoruban forest, Sahael

The Yoruba Forest, also known as the Black Wood, was a dark, elaborate labyrinth of dead ends, twists, and time loops. Adewara warned them that the forest had long been known to confuse infuriate travelers who strayed from the paths. Over the next four days, Aamira couldn't tell if they were making progress or simply traveling in one big circle. The thick foliage above often blocked out the sun for hours. Luckily, animals and wild game were plentiful, allowing them to eat well and sleep safely in branches above the moist ground.

There was no fruit on any of the trees, however, something that made Aamira think that not all life had been restored to these lands.

An unnatural fatigue set in as they traveled. Aamira's head throbbed, as did her joints. They searched for any sign of a trail or roadway but found nothing. At times they would find themselves arguing about which direction to take, or who knew more about wilderness survival. Lanae would start singing randomly in the middle of a song before stopping herself without completing the melody. Occasionally they would come across large cobwebs that hung lifeless in the still air.

"I hate it here," Yinká said on the evening of their sixth day in the forest.

"That's the tenth time you've said that today," Lanae spat. "We don't need to hear it again."

"I'm hungry," Yinká replied. "We should kill one of the wildebeest we say in the clearing earlier today. That would fill me up."

Abioye touched a dried flower bud as they passed and crushed it between his fingers. "Does anyone else think it's strange that while the trees and animals are all alive, all the flowers are still dead?"

"I hadn't noticed," Yinká replied.

"I had," Aamira answered. "Two days ago, we came upon that grove, but all the flowers were black."

"I thought that's the type of flowers they were," Yinká said.

"There are no insects either," Adewara added.

"What do you mean?" Abioye asked.

"Well, we've seen wildebeest, jaguars, birds, evidence of spiders, but no bees, flies, wasps, or mosquitos. No fruit on the trees either. Plus, I haven't seen any white short-haired bears. You'll remember from our studies back in Karnak when you were first married, the short-haired bears act as protectors of the Yoruban Forest. They wander, keeping out intruders. From what I understand, they are quite common, and yet I haven't seen a single one during our journey. It's as if only certain substrates of life in Sahael have been revived. Without the flowers and insects, fruit for the herbivores, eventually the life that has been restored will naturally die again. Without the bears, and the soldiers that would ride them, there will be no protection from danger to travelers.

This feels more like a temporary revival instead of a lasting rebirth, at least until the other forms of life are returned."

"I'm more than happy to not have the mosquitoes---" Yinká began.

"Quiet," Adewara said as he stopped in front of the group. He held his arms wide as if protecting them from danger.

"What is it, Adewara?" Aamira asked.

The Educator held up his finger and pointed to a single tight strand of silvery twine.

"Cryptic Stick Spider," he whispered.

"We've come across webs before," Abioye said.

Adewara shook his head. "Fresh," he whispered, touching the strand lightly.

As if in response to the slight vibration, the trees above rustled with activity. Aamira looked up into the dark branches. A few streams of sunlight poked through the canopy. She saw movement, and what looked like something with long legs.

Holding his finger over his mouth, Adewara side-stepped the web and led the group toward a clearing.

"I hate it here," Yinká repeated.

Just as he said the words, the young man stepped on something that gave an angry bellow. A wildebeest had apparently been resting hidden in the ferns until Yinká accidentally stepped on its leg. The hairy creature reared up and howled.

Several similar howls answered the first.

Aamira turned, seeing a group of at least ten wildebeests charging through the trees. At the same moment, a spiderweb shot from above, hitting the back of the first animal.

"Run!" Adewara ordered.

The group turned and plunged to the side. The Wildebeests charged at them with no regard for the spiders and their traps. Arachnids the size of large dogs dropped from the canopy and shot webs at the rampaging animals. Several wildebeests tried to change course but found themselves suddenly webbed and incapacitated.

The Stick spiders subdued them one by one before climbing on their backs and plunging their fangs into thick flesh.

"Leaf snakes!" Lanae cried as large serpents slithered out of the brush toward the fighting wildebeests. Aamira leaped over a snake to keep from being bitten.

"Hate it here!" Yinká shouted as they ran.

"Shut up!" Lanae shouted back.

Leaves slapped Aamira's face as she charged through the forest at top speed. Out of the corner of her eye she saw a web splatter against a tree not five feet from her.

"The spiders are following us!" Adewara yelled.

The ground seemed to disappear beneath Aamira's feet without warning as it sloped sharply into a ravine. She fell forward and smashed through brush and vines until finally landing on her back in a puddle. Abioye fell beside her, with Yinká, Lanae, and Adewara coming to a stop not far away.

"Is everybody okay?" Abioye groaned as he pushed himself up.

"I'm pretty scratched up, but otherwise fine," Aamira answered.

"Now we have to climb out of here," Yinká grumbled.

A deep, guttural grunt caught Aamira's ear as she stood. The bass tone vibrated the air around them with its resonance. The trees in the ravine shook with the movement of something large.

Out of the vegetation stomped an enormous, pale, ten-foot-tall ape. The monster roared and snorted, as if the intruders had just interrupted a nap.

Just as Aamira thought to form swords in her hands, Inkalamu's Heart began to glow green, just as it had on the water almost a week before. The ape paused and stepped back.

"Mother, look," Yinká said, pointing up.

Aamira looked toward the tops of the trees, seeing a dozen Stick Spiders hanging overhead. None of the creatures moved, all seemingly transfixed by the jewel around her neck.

Then, without any protest, the ape and the spiders retreated calmly, returning to the depths of the forest.

"We knew Inkalamu's Heart would be necessary for our journey to Sahael," Adewara breathed, "but even I was unaware of how integral it would be to our survival."

Aamira touched the stone around her neck, remembering when the two halves were given to her by Sariah and Oxossi. Sariah had said, *Inkalamu's Heart consists of many Emerald pieces needed to help restore what's been lost in Neros's Realm and Sahael. Each of your family members is worthy of one of the six stones, as you earned them in your trials.*

Those words were proving truer by the day.

As they walked through the rest of the evening, the Heart continued glowing.

"Inkalamu's Heart seems to grow brighter as we turn north," Aamira said. "At least, I think it's north in the failing light."

"Does that mean anything?" Abioye asked. "It wasn't glowing before. Not until the animals tried to kill us."

Aamira looked around. "I think it's trying to guide us somewhere."

They hiked through the brush for another hour. Darkness fell all around them, but the light from the gems illuminated their path. As Aamira had thought, the Heart glowed brighter depending on which direction they took, until eventually they reached a clearing under bright stars and a moonless night. There in the center of the meadow stood twelve tall statues of imposing stone; six men and six women, all in the posture of praying.

"The Yoruban royal house," Adewara said in awe. "These statues are ancient."

"Look at the eyes, Father," Lanae breathed.

A pale green glow emanated from the statue's eyes. As Aamira walked closer, the glow intensified. Gemstones similar to Inkalamu's Heart were embedded in the stone like piercing irises.

"They're reacting to the Heart," Abioye said.

Aamira focused on the statues. One of them, a towering woman with braided hair, had only one glowing eye. Looking down at the Heart, Aamira noticed that one of the six pieces making up the stone glowed brighter than the others.

Removing the piece of crystal, Aamira climbed up the statue until she looked the stone woman face to face. She took the gem and placed it in the dead socket.

It was an exact match.

When the emerald piece was placed in the right eye socket, an emerald mist spewed from the mouths of the twelve giant statues. The fog spread throughout the forest.

After a few minutes, the group stood under the stars waiting for something to happen. Eventually the soil absorbed the mist and all was still.

"So, what did that do?" Yinká asked.

"I don't know," Aamira admitted.

Just then, a buzzing sound reached Aamira's ear. She swatted at something in the darkness.

"It's a bee!" Adewara shouted.

Soon, the sound of crickets filled the forest, along with the scratching of other insects. Only now with the natural song of life once again abundant could Aamira fully appreciate how quiet the forest had been during their trek.

"One more link in the natural world restored," Adewara smiled.

The five of them continued traveling another week, eventually making their way out of the labyrinthine forest. They continued north along a ridgeline that allowed them to see more of the land. Green fields stretched off in every direction, with the Yoruba Forest to the south. That afternoon, Inkalamu's Heart began glowing again, pointing them slightly west along the cliffs.

That evening, a large thunderstorm dropped heavy rain on the travelers. Cold winds blew. Finding a cave along one of the cliffs, they took shelter for the night. The Heart never ceased shining.

"I'll take the first watch," Adewara said. "We're all tired. I'll start a fire, and you can all rest."

As night crept on, Aamira and Abioye sat together near the warm embers, sharing the second watch together. Aamira rubbed her rings and bracelet, as if they would somehow recapture the past.

"What's wrong?' Abioye asked.

"My heart is heavy; I miss our children."

"They'll be fine on Sentinel Island," Abioye soothed. "They're grown men, after all. Once they get to Sahaeland, it will all be new to them. A whole new life. Plus, we have Yinká with us. He looks enough like his brothers, I'm surprised you miss them at all."

"It's not that," Aamira replied. "I miss them when they were children. Even Yinká is a man now. I miss their little feet and incessant questions. I feel lately like I've been mourning for the life we could never give them. I mean, they grew up in a realm where time only passed for them. Imagine what that would have been like. Yes, we interacted with people and made friends during that time, but those folks always returned to the same pattern of action no matter what we did. I remember when Yekú had that crush on the palace chef's daughter. He would go and learn recipes all day just so he could be close to her. Then one afternoon he realized she was staying the same age as he kept growing older. It was heartbreaking."

"Not for me," Abioye shrugged. "Without that experience, Yekú never would have learned to cook the way he has. You realize how many good meals I would have missed out on?"

Laughter filled the cave as the couple snuggled closer.

"Our boys are strong men," Abioye assured. "And we're a strong couple. We haven't always been, but we are now."

Aamira and Abioye talked for another hour, when a strange grumbling sound echoed in the cave. Aamira looked to see if the others were startled awake by the noise, but they all slept soundly.

"What was that?" Abioye whispered.

"I don't know," Aamira said, sitting up. "We should take a look. I don't want any surprises pushing us back into the rain."

The two of them crept into the darkness, relying on their

enhanced vision to guide them. Inkalamu's Heart continued glowing green with enough power to accent the contours of the cave. Warm air blew in their faces the deeper they delved. A smell of animal dander wafted with the breeze.

"There is something down here. I can smell it," Abioye breathed.

A low grumble could be heard in the stillness of the cavern.

"I can hear whatever it is," Aamira replied quietly.

Within moments they came upon a pile of hibernating white short-haired bears, all lumped together for warmth. Aamira counted at least a dozen, but it looked as if many more huddled behind the first mass. Strangely, a green mist wafted around the bears, twisting on air currents and circling the creatures as if sentient.

"What's that fog?" Abioye asked.

"I don't know."

Looking more closely, Aamira noticed a large black spider crawling along the fur of one of the bears. The arachnid crept up to the bear's face, where a web had been spun around the creature's nose. The bear seemed completely oblivious.

"Something's not right here," Aamira said. "I don't know much about bears, but I'm sure they wouldn't normally let a spider make a web on their face and up their nose even in deep hibernation."

"You think it's something magical? Adewara mentioned last week about how there weren't any bears in the forest."

Stepping forward, Aamira held her hand out and touched the swirling mist. Instantly she lost all feeling in her fingers. Cold crept up her arm.

"The fog is keeping them asleep," she said. "I'm sure of it.

I can feel the sluggishness and fatigue in my hand."

"What can we do to help these sleeping animals?" Abioye asked. "The white short-haired bears share the responsibility of protecting the Yoruban Forest. I remember reading about them in Karnak. If they're all asleep here, there are none patrolling the forest, just as Adewara feared."

The cold continued spreading up Aamira's arm, but as soon as it drew to her shoulder, Inkalamu's Heart glowed brighter than before. Warmth extended from Aamira's chest, filling her veins with healing comfort.

"Inkalamu's Heart is the key," Aamira said. She removed the necklace, looking at the remaining crystal pieces.

"What do we do?" Abioye asked. "Do we throw it in the mist? When you touched the jewel to the water, it healed the soil and revitalized the dry trees. Maybe that's all you need to do this time too."

That didn't feel right to Aamira. She walked around the sleeping bears, avoiding the fog as best she could. Then, on her right, the light from the Heart glistened on a metal symbol of the Yoruban sigil; a short-faced bear's face in a stylized circle.

The sigil's eyes were missing.

"Here," she said, pointing at the symbol.

"Will it take two pieces of the Heart since it's missing both eyes?" Abioye questioned.

"Only one way to find out."

Aamira removed two chunks of crystal like pulling apart a magnet. Each piece fit into the eyes of the symbol. The sigil lit up with a green hue. Instantly, the mist sunk into the ground as if sucked by an enormous breath.

Several bears snorted and began to stir.

"They're waking up," Abioye smiled. "Do you think they're dangerous?"

"Not to us." Aamira stepped over to one of the bears as the creature climbed to its four legs and shook its head back and forth as if casting off a groggy slumber. She petted the bear's soft fur.

"I remember these bears. When I was a little girl, it was short-haired bears that helped save me and my cousins on the day Sahael was captured. We hid in a similar cave like this when we left Khartoum Palace before being loaded on the slave ships."

Another bear, this one far larger than the others, stepped forward and bowed to Aamira. He was massive; large enough to ride like a horse.

"He likes you," Abioye said.

The bear nudged Aamira's legs, as if trying to lift her off the ground.

"I think he wants you to climb on. Adewara said soldiers would ride them into battle, so maybe that's what this big guy wants."

"I'll try it," Aamira said as she grabbed the bear's hair and flung her leg over the animal. The bear's warm body rose higher as the beast stood and roared. Other bears moved forward, one nudging Abioye.

"Climb on that one," Aamira said. "They're very calm and docile."

"Yeah, right now they are," Abioye said as he mounted the bear. "I'd hate to face one of these in a fight."

The group of bears moved through the dark toward the entrance of the cave. Aamira looked back, seeing hundreds of bears, possibly thousands.

"There's so many," she gasped.

As the bears approached the exit, Aamira saw Adewara, Lanae, and Yinká standing in front of the rainy night, shocked and confused.

"What's going on?" Adewara shouted as several bears ran past him into the fresh air.

"Climb on!" Aamira cried. "The bears are here to help!"

The others found bears of their own and within minutes were riding into the night. The rain was cold, but the warmth from the bears seemed to insulate Aamira from the worst of the discomfort. Most of the bears disappeared into the forest, while the four mounts continued north.

By dawn, Aamira calculated they had traveled at least 25 miles; more than they would have traversed in an entire day on foot.

After only one day of traveling at speed, the four travelers arrived at the gates to Sahael itself. The Sahaelian symbol of the Marula Tree adorned the orichalcum barrier which stood two hundred feet tall.

"How do we get past the gate?" Yinká asked as he patted his bear's back.

Aamira dismounted and looked at the towering barrier. Pride swelled in her chest as she appreciated the skill of her ancestors in the creation of such impressive gates. The symbols of each of the royal houses adorned the surface.

"Why isn't it open?" Abioye asked. "If Oadira, or one of the other princesses made their way here and started the reclamation of Sahael, why would the gate still be closed?"

"There are other ways into the Crater of Sahael and the capital cities," Adewara stated. "Particularly from the north. This is the official southern entrance. And if they came this way, they may have closed the gate behind them. We have no way of knowing."

Placing her hand against the smooth surface of the gate, Aamira felt the thrill of having made it this far. In response to her touch, the Yoruban sigil lit up, allowing the large two-hundred-foot-tall gates to open. A gust of wind blew through, tossing her braids about.

And then Aamira took her first step into the city of her childhood. The bears waited at the gate, as if ready to accept any order they were given.

Over the next hour they wandered the streets, looking up at broken buildings and cratered streets. Skeletons littered the ground, some wearing Sahaelian armor, others that of Narsans and Ennead. The battle had obviously been fierce on that terrible day of death. Nitrate bombs had done extensive damage everywhere. Vines grew on the debris, water flowing along broken gutters and tumbling like waterfalls from shattered aqueducts.

"This place has seen better days," Yinká said as he picked up a broken cobblestone and tossed it aside.

"We should make our way to Khartoum Palace," Adewara said.

"Do you know the way, Father?" Lanae asked.

"It's been many decades, but I've set foot in this city more times than I can count. I know the way."

They walked to the destroyed palace doors of Khartoum Palace, which hung from broken hinges. The roof had completely collapsed, with most of the walls crumbling with time. Limited memories flashed in Aamira's mind, but she did remember those doors.

"I remember some of this," she said, touching the brass handles that guards would pull on to open the doors. She pointed to the right toward a series of toppled columns. "There was a garden over here, wasn't there? We were playing there when the attack started."

"That's the Yoruban courtyard," Adewara explained.

They walked through what remained of the garden. Weeds sprouted everywhere, growing among the bones and skulls. Adewara led them into the palace from there, pointing out what remained of beautiful tile murals and statues that were now little more than chunks of marble. Aamira stepped into the middle of where the four bloodlines would converge among the Nabtahenge Gates. She looked at the floor covered in rubble and glass from the ceiling that once protected her ancestors from the elements. The remains of a white Rhino skeleton slumped against one of the walls.

"Wait," Adewara said, holding his hand in front of Aamira. "Look at the stones here."

Aamira could tell that the area where the Nabtahenge Gates had dropped into the stone floor had been cleared of debris. In fact, some of the stones looked as though they had been lifted by the gates themselves.

"This gate has been activated," Adewara grinned.

Suddenly the ground shook and the stones of the Nabtahenge Gate began rising from the floor. They emerged, glowing with electricity, until they towered above them in a circle pattern.

"Step back!" Adewara ordered.

The group jumped over the debris and looked back as a portal opened. Air rushed in and blew violently for a moment. Then, three people stepped from the portal. Adewara cried out as a beautiful woman with dark skin and braided hair pulled back in a ponytail stepped forward.

"My love!" Adewara wept as he raced into the center to hug and kiss the woman.

"Mother!" Lanae shouted.

Lyshyla the Educator. Aamira knew it had to be Adewara's wife, the one he had kept secret from her and her sons for so many years. Adewara and his wife sobbed openly as they embraced, crying for the decades they hadn't seen each other. Lanae hugged them both at the same time as the knelt on the ground in joy.

It was then that Aamira noticed the other two individuals standing in the light. One was a handsome young man, tall and broad, wearing the garb of a king. She didn't know who he was. He looked very important, though he couldn't be much older than Yinká.

The other man she recognized immediately, even after 30 years.

"Solomon!" Aamira shouted. She rushed toward the bald man in his green robes. Solomon laughed and embraced Aamira.

"You made it, my little Yoruban," he whispered into her ear. "I am so proud of you."

Tears flowed from Aamira's eyes. She wept freely. A weight lifted off her shoulders that had rested there since the Royal Rumble decades before when Solomon had first told Aamira and her cousins about their calling to redeem Sahael. The weight had grown as she matured and truly began to understand what it meant. And now, after journeying to the Sand Lands of IFF, Neros's Realm, sailing halfway around Aarde, traveling dark tunnels, and raising a family, she finally stood in her homeland, embraced by the protector of Aarde himself.

"I made it," Aamira cried. "I made it."

"And not alone, I assume," Solomon said as he pulled from the embrace. "Ancient writing say the queen of the Yoruban line will arrive in Sahael with a hundred thousand people behind her. Please tell me that's the case."

Aamira turned back toward the others. Abioye and Yinká stood there smiling, while Adewara, Lyshyla, and Lanae continued embracing.

"We brought lots of ships with us," Aamira admitted. "A full fleet of 100 ships all packed to the brim with people. But many of the vessels were lost in a storm before we crashed on the Sentinel Islands. We're not sure what happened to them. We had Yorubans, Orishans, Lysinnians, Romans, Rysallians, and black albino Demirrians with us."

"I'm sure they will be accounted for. Since the land has been made habitable once more, people that land or crash on shore will be able to survive easily enough. We will find them." Solomon then motioned toward the kingly young man next to him. "May I introduce King Onika of the Orishan bloodline, fourth son of Oadira."

"Oadira!" Aamira shouted happily. "Is she here? Where is she?"

"My mother and father are not in the capital city at the moment," King Onika said as he stepped forward. "They are in the city of Sahaedron to the north. Part of the rebirth of Sahael that my mother set into motion was the promised revival of the people in that city that had died in Natas's attack. Unfortunately, the people were heavily divided at that time, and upon being brought back to life, continued to be divided and argue over silly political nonsense. My parents are working to unify them while rebuilding the city, otherwise this continent will simply fall again when eventually challenged."

Adewara came to his feet and bowed. "King Onika. It is an honor. I apologize for my emotions."

"Don't apologize, Adewara," Aamira said. "You haven't seen your wife in probably 40 years by my count. You can have a moment to be human like the rest of us."

"Their sacrifice has not been in vain," Solomon said. "I visited them on Inheritance several years after the fall of Sahael and called them to this duty. I promised them their separation would feel like but a moment once they were reunited, and their lives would be so long that it would barely be remembered. I hope my promise has proven true."

"It has," Adewara cried. He smiled and kissed his wife again.

Solomon stepped toward Yinká, hand out in a welcoming gesture. "And you must be High King Yinká. It is an honor to meet you, young man. The whisperings of the spirit of Ishtar and Obatala have mentioned your name, and that you would be guided to this moment."

"Thank you…Solomon, Protector of Aarde," Yinká said with some hesitation.

"We will make sure you and your fellow king get better acquainted," Solomons said. "King Onika, would you take your fellow sovereign through the portal and get him some food? The rest of us still have a few things to accomplish before we join you. There are still things needing to be done."

"Of course, Solomon."

Onika and Yinká stepped through the portal and disappeared in the white electricity.

"I don't understand why Yinká had to leave," Aamira said.

"The remainder of our work for the Yoruban bloodline must be performed by their queen," Solomon said. "Follow me."

Aamira, Abioye, Adewara, Lyshyla, and Lanae walked through the Yoruban halls behind Solomon. Sunlight streamed through holes in the ceiling. They stepped around debris that littered the once pristine tiles. Skeletons lay all around.

"We haven't had the chance to clean things up here yet," Solomon said as they walked. "Oadira and her husband Ozias didn't arrive that long ago, and before that of course, Alkebulan could not be inhabited. It will require an army of workers to demolish and rebuild Sahael. Right now, our focus has been on Sahaedron, since that people were brought back to serve in that exact capacity."

The group entered what remained of a grand hall. Pillars had collapsed along with sections of the stone wall. Solomon pointed to a large symbol on the wall of an eye with a stylized flourish sweeping off from the bottom eyelashes. Beside it Aamira noticed the Orishan symbol, filled with two sapphire stones, but the Hausan and the Demirrian characters next to it were not yet filled.

"Behold the Eye of NeRu," Solomon said. "The Eye of NeRu is made of Orichalcum and was built into the wall of the Sahaelian House, the Sahaelian senate chambers, the Sahaelian commons, and the Sahaelian court. As you can see, this one is of the Yoruban bloodline and is missing two large circular crystal pieces to become operational once more."

Aamira looked down at what remained of Inkalamu's Heart. She took a piece and handed it to Abioye, while grasping the other herself. They climbed up a large section of broken wall to NeRu's eye. Placing each crystal in its place, the symbol began to glow brightly.

Suddenly, Aamira could see through the eyes of every animal in the Yoruban Forest and throughout all Aarde. She felt their fear, freedom, hunger, lust, anger, all of it. Animalistic emotion flowed through her as all animal life connected to her mind. She simultaneously ran through a jungle, leaped from a tree, ate her prey, and fell prey to a predator in a single instant.

"You can now see through the eyes of all of the animals on

Aarde, just like the Yoruban royal family could before the fall of Sahael," Solomon said.

The connection faded, and Aamira took a deep breath. She knew that if she wanted, she could open her mind to any animal and see through its eyes. She had connected with the minds of animals before, but never to a scale even close to this.

Adewara stepped forward and helped Aamira and Abioye step down from the rubble.

"Can we use NeRu's Eye to see things around Aarde now?" Abioye asked. "I've read it has the power to see all creation."

"We can only use the eye once the four bloodlines have returned to Sahael," Adewara said. "Only the four bloodlines have access to it. No one else is permitted to use it unless they've been found and accounted for. Only you can use it."

"These lenses that make up NeRu's eye were used to help the rulers of Sahael mobilize their people throughout their home world," Solomon informed. "From Khartoum Palace they could mobilize people, armies, and resources throughout Aarde to help wherever needed no matter the circumstances. Sahael is to be the mediator between the four realms, deciding how to take care of Alkebulan and help all people get back to Ishtar and Obatala in Andalusia."

"So once my other two cousins arrive in Sahael, we'll be able to search all Aarde for people in need?" Aamira asked.

"Yes," Solomon nodded. "Now, we have another stop at the Necrosis Chamber where your ancestors are buried. Follow me once more."

Solomon led them deeper into the ruins of Khartoum. In one intersection hallway, the bones of hundreds of people littered the ground. They descended a staircase that led underground where more skeletons lay unceremoniously rotting. At one point on the stairs Abioye accidentally stepped on a skull and crushed it.

"The Ennead spared no one," Lyshyla said. She and Adewara held hands. It was strange to see Adewara so happy and relaxed. For 30 years he had wrapped himself in a constant air of stress like a blanket. Now he seemed to have cast it off in the presence of his wife.

The hallway grew darker as they progressed further underground. Solomon waved his hand and balls of blue light appeared, illuminating the path.

Upon arriving at the entrance of the burial chamber, a circular Nabta door blocked the way. The shiny black stone was covered in dust, accenting the intricate carvings and symbols across its surface.

"We need a key to enter the burial chamber," Lyshyla said. "An emerald key. Oadira did not obtain anything of this nature on our journey. Did you, Queen Aamira, perhaps find anything like this as you traveled to Sahael?"

"Yes," Aamira replied. "But we don't have it. This reminds me of Nzingha's Emerald key that was taken from Neros's realm by Captain Brooks and second commander Geb of the Ennead legion. They entered Neros's realm and took what they wanted years before the assault on Sahael. They killed my grandparents."

"Is there any other way to get in?" Abioye asked.

"It is spoken that the queen of the Yoruban line can open the door," Solomon said.

Looking at the barrier, Aamira shrugged. "Perhaps, I can use the second-to-last piece of Inkalamu's Heart." She turned to Solomon. "All of this was prophesied, right? That means circumstances should converge to allow things to happen; things that couldn't have been planned."

Lyshyla nodded to Solomon. "That's what happened with

Oadira and Nassir's sapphire obelisk. Natas destroyed the holy relic by smashing it in his anger. When we arrived here, there was no water. Water couldn't even exist within the boundaries of the Sahaelian capital city. And yet one of Natas's blows left a gouge that fit the last piece of Okavango's Heart perfectly. We healed the realm because circumstances created the exact path for us to follow."

"Wait, there are two crystal hearts?" Abioye asked.

Adewara rubbed his forehead. "I've taught you this before."

"Don't be embarrassed," Abioye smiled. "Most of the time I only listen to half of what you're saying anyway."

At the top of the Nabta gate Aamira saw a carving of a soldier holding a sword. The small blade looked to have been cut more deeply than the other artwork. Could it be the right size?

"Lift me up so I can reach the top," Aamira said.

Abioye hoisted his wife up and she placed Inkalamu's emerald piece inside the empty slot. Within a few seconds, the Nabta door dissipated like fog, allowing entrance into Necrosis's Chamber.

Solomon grinned and stepped forward through the round opening. Aamira followed, seeing a large burial room filled with ornate sarcophagi. Unlike the rest of the ruined palace, this room seemed completely undisturbed. It was far enough underground that it had not been damaged in the bombings, nor had it been breached by Natas's forces.

"The first Ancient Kemites of Sahael and the chosen bloodlines share this burial chamber," Solomon said. "It's divided into fourths, with doors on separate entrances."

"Before the first Supremes died, they wanted to help establish the four realms and Sahael for the people of Alkebulan,"

Adewara informed "Lyshyla and I were summoned to Sahael to help with one of the three responsibilities."

"What are the three responsibilities?" Aamira asked. She had never heard Adewara speak of any specific obligations before.

"Their three responsibilities consisted of defending and serving the people of Alkebulan," Solomon said, "watching over the fours realms, and keeping a close eye on Sahael."

The group walked to the center of the room, where a single pillar held up the ceiling. The pilar had been carved to look like a massive Iroku tree, with roots reaching into the ground and branches holding up the heavens.

"The tree represents Alkebulan," Solomon said. "It is Iroku, the Yoruban Tree, or Tree of Life. Each branch on the Yoruba tree represents the twelve tribes of Alkebulan that were lost and scattered in different locations all over Aarde. The lower trunk consists of the three chosen bloodlines. From the trunk, twelve additional branches represent the ancient bloodlines of Sahael. The roots have three large branches, each representing the Songhai Dynasty, the Axum Dynasty, and the Kush Dynasty."

"It's a beautiful carving," Aamira replied. "I'm glad it survived the destruction of the palace."

"After the fall of Sahael," Solomon continued, "the chosen bloodlines were enslaved and scattered all over Aarde by the Narsans. The ancient bloodlines had the responsibility to make Sahael the protector of all people but fell into petty disputes and pride. Due to philosophical differences, the four realms closed themselves off to Sahael, Alkebulan, and Aarde. It was not until Sahael started feeling the presence of white darkness in Aarde that the ruling class decided to act, and by then it was too late."

"It wasn't until the signs of the times gave you and your cousins the urge and burning desire to return to Alkebulan that the true purpose of Sahael began to reassert itself," Lyshyla said, touching the carved pillar reverently.

"The Marula Tree represents the heartbeat of Sahael," Adewara said. "This pillar holds great power and purpose for all people. That is why Solomon brought us here."

"It is," Solomon agreed. "The four bloodlines represented Life Magic, Life Energy, Spirit Energy, and Necromancy. When the other chosen tribes arrived, the remaining tribes could use their Artes and powers only within Sahael to help and serve the Alkebulan people, for it was written in The Nairobi Laws."

"Why are we here in this chamber?" Aamira asked.

"We need to place the last piece of Inkalamu's Heart in the center of Necrosis's Chamber," Lyshyla answered.

"Where? I see no slot to place this last piece," Aamira said.

"This you must figure out on your own," Adewara said.

Aamira rubbed her hand along the pillar's surface. Several slots had been carved, one in the shape of a key.

"That is where Nzinga's Onyx key was once housed," Lyshyla informed. "It was lost some time in the last century."

Feeling with her finger, Aamira noticed a slot about the size of her pinky. Knowing that the last piece of the Heart needed to be placed somewhere on the carved column, without a word she pulled the last chunk from the necklace and slipped it into the gap.

"I think that will work," she breathed.

Part of the twisted stone trunk began to glow green and light up a section of branches in the ceiling. The light moved along the carved rock above, pulsing until it seemed almost absorbed by the stone.

"You have enlivened the Yoruban bloodline," Solomon beamed. "As prophesied, the dead Yorubans here in the capital city will be revived as the Orishans of Sahaedron were by your cousin several months ago. Oh, blessed day of rejoicing! Ishtar and Obatala be praised!"

Abioye sidled next to Aamira and whispered in her ear. "What is he talking about? Is he saying people are going to be brought back from the dead?"

The question was answered almost immediately as a flash of light drew their attention back to the dark hallway through which they had entered. Aamira ran to the entrance and saw tendrils of material like quick growing vines wrapped around several skeletons in the corridor. Flesh began to form around the bone, until two men and three women had completely rematerialized on the floor.

"What is going on?" Abioye gasped in disbelief.

"The revitalization of Sahael," Adewara replied.

The newly alive Yorubans stood naked, looking at their limbs as if unsure how they lived once again. Lyshyla pulled off her cloak and wrapped it around the nearest woman.

"What is…where?" the woman asked.

"It's okay," Lyshyla soothed. "You're alive once more. The pain you remember is just a nightmare now. The queens of Sahael are returning."

Adewara and Abioye removed their cloaks as well to help cover the nakedness of their kin.

Moving quickly, Solomon stepped past them.

"Come," he said. "Let us head to the surface and see what has been redeemed."

The group ran up the stairs toward the collapsed palace. They encountered several more revived and confused people on the steps.

Aamira looked at the remaining skeletons that lay all around undisturbed. "Why are only some of the people being brought back to life?"

"Only the Yorubans," Solomon replied without slowing his step toward the surface. "And only here in the capital. Rebirth is in many ways a sacrifice, not a blessing. Death is not the empty darkness that most mortals fear it to be. The blessings of a life well lived reverberate into eternity, just as the emptiness of a selfish existence creates more emptiness for that person. We create our futures in both the physical and spiritual realm. We create our joys or sorrows. For the people who died here fighting to protect their families and neighbors, while they won't remember their time in the eternal realm, coming back to life will be met with a twinge of sorrow. They will know they are here for a glorious purpose, to serve others, but will still long to see the loved ones they left behind. Such are feelings that men like Natas and his followers will never experience. 'Tis tragedy."

They reached the surface and all around stood living members of the Yoruban house. Hundreds of people blinked in the sunlight, puzzled. Some of them spoke to each other in whispered tones, trying to figure out what happened to them and the city around them.

Raising his hands above his head, Solomon performed a series of hand gestures. Green mist then flowed up from the ground and encircled the naked Yorubans, forming clothing to cover their bodies.

"That's a good trick," Abioye smiled.

The people looked at Solomon, their eyes suddenly glowing with emerald power. Aamira's eyes and tattoos lit up as well.

"There is magical energy in Sahael once more," Lyshyla said with a sigh of relief.

"What does that mean?" Aamira asked as her eyes sparkled and shined Zambian.

Adewara closed his eyes and took a deep breath. "It means that Nier's realm now has magic energy running through it once more. Magical energy is making its way back to Sahael."

Over the next several hours, tens of thousands of Yorubas made their way to the ruins of Khartoum Palace. They laughed and cheered. Aamira greeted as many as she could with Abioye by her side. In the evening, Yinká and Onika returned through the Nabtahenge Gate. Yinká now wore kingly robes of creamy white with gold accents. Aamira and Abioye hugged their son and cried.

"Your brothers are never going to let you live this down. You know that, right?" Abioye chuckled.

"They'll get over it," Yinká smiled.

As the sun set, a massive crowd gathered in what remained of Khartoum Square beside the palace. From the throng of Yorubans, a young girl and boy stepped forward and started to chant the phrase:

"Swing low, sweet chariot."

Then the crowd began to sing the words along with the children until thousands of voices rang out in shouted praise.

"Coming for to carry me home."

"I looked over Sahael, and what did I see."

"Coming for to carry me home."

"A band of angels coming after me"

"Coming for to carry me home."

"Swing Low, sweet chariot."

"Coming for to carry me home."

"Swing low, sweet chariot."

"Coming for to carry me home."

"If you get there before I do."

"Coming for to carry me home."

"If you get there before I do."

"Coming for to carry me home."

"Tell all my Yorubans I'm coming too."

"Coming for to carry me home."

"Swing low, sweet chariot."

"Coming for to carry me home."

"Swing low, sweet chariot."

"Please come to take us to Sahaeland."

They pumped their fists to the sky in unison and roared a cheer of gratitude.

Aamira wiped tears from her eyes. Yes, the city was still destroyed, but her people lived once more. Soon word would be sent to her other sons and they would bring the Rysallians and Romans with them to their new homeland.

Peace would reign.

At least, that's what she hoped.

Two weeks had passed by the time news of their sons reached Aamira and Abioye. Local Yoruban ship builders had found two old fishing vessels they had been contructing before their deaths in a cave port that had survived the attack years ago.

They sailed quickly to the unified Sentinel Island. Aamira's sons sent letters back informing their parents that they had chosen to continue leading their respective groups to the cities in the north as promised before meeting them in the capital city of Sahael. The news brought sadness and pride to Aamira's heart. She wanted to see her three other sons but respected their choice to stand firm in their duty. Ryland, Ryal, and Rashida had returned with the boats however, and had spent the full day since their arrival sequestered with Solomon. Word had also reached the capital that most of the ships from their armada had either crashed or landed safely on the shores of Alkebulan. Messengers had been sent to guide them to the appropriate cities where Yekú, Yomí, and Yemí would organize them for reconstruction duties.

Work had begun in rebuilding Sahael itself. The Yorubans who had been brought back to life divided into crews and started gathering human remains and preparing them for burial. The bodies of any Narsan or Ennead soldiers were being burned outside the city and would receive no honor in death. After the cleansing was completed, the people would begin removing debris and reconstructing Khartoum Palace and the surrounding area. It would take years, but time was on their side.

On the afternoon of the second day since the sailor's return with Ryland, Ryal, and Rashida, Lyshyla found Aamira and her team in the city center as she organized burial efforts for the desiccated Sahaelian bodies throughout the city.

"Empress Adesola," the Educator bowed. "Solomon has requested you and your husband's presence in the meeting hall of Khartoum."

"I'm not sure where Abioye is right now," Aamira replied before handing a map of areas to cleanse to one of her assistants.

"Adewara is seeking out your husband, so all should be well."

The two women walked silently toward the palace remains.
Finally, Aamira spoke.

"When will I get to see Oadira? We've been here for two
weeks. I know the gates are open between the cities. I'd like to see
my cousin after so many years."

"Solomon is coordinating a time," Lyshyla said. "Things in
Sahaedron are fraught at the moment. Rebuilding goes slowly
because the people still hold to their old grievances. Oadira has
been made aware of your arrival and is excited to see you as well,
but she wants to spend some time with you, not merely have a brief
interaction. They are trying to get everything worked out for that to
happen."

Disappointment filled Aamira's chest with her next breath.
She would be content to see Oadira for five minutes if that's all she
could get but understood her own responsibilities well enough to
appreciate Oadira's.

People waved and called out as the two women passed by.
A young girl ran up and handed Aamira some fresh fruit that had
just been picked from the orchards. Aamira thanked the girl and
waved to the food carts that had been set up to feed the workers.

"You're doing a good job leading the people," Lyshyla
said.

"Thank you. Your husband taught me well about how to
administrate and work with people."

"He is a good man," Lyshyla smiled.

"It would have been nice to know about your existence
earlier," Aamira replied. "We only found out Adewara was
married a year or two ago. My sons took it pretty hard that he had
kept that from them."

Lyshyla nodded and pursed her lips as if trying to find the

right words to say.

"If it makes you feel any better," Lyshyla began, "I never told Oadira and her family that I was married either. It may sound selfish, but even thinking about it brought great pain to me. I had to cut myself off from that part of my life, otherwise I would be overcome with loneliness and grief. I know for a fact my husband felt the same way."

"It makes sense," Aamira responded.

And it did make sense. For years, she and Abioye's relationship had been little more than cursory words and occasional glances. Now however they were strong and truly in love. Being without him would be incredibly difficult. How would she cope with being apart from him for 40 years?

They entered the palace through one of the broken walls and found Solomon standing in front of the silent Nabtahenge Gates. He wore a black cloak and hood that obscured his face. Ryland, Ryal, Rashida, Adewara, and Abioye stood in front of him.

"Welcome, Aamira," he said. "We have a few things to discuss as a group."

"I'm interested in anything you have to tell me, Solomon, protector of Aarde," Aamira replied.

"Your three sons are in need of your help," he began. "Sahaeland is in need of saving. It is time to get your Kingdom in order. The Romans Dodecahedron needs the eight spheres from the eight islands of Burgundian, Herulian, Lombard, Gepid, Alamannian, Frisian, Frankish, and the Anglo-Saxon Kingdoms."

"Are we then to seek out those spheres?" Aamira asked.

"No. Augustus Ryal and Augusta Rashida to travel to their ancestral homeland of Rome. In time, their first-born child will be the Caesar that helps fill the Roman Dodecahedron from the eight nations needing to be brought under one Caesar. Since Ryal is witan and Rashida black, their child will be the bridge between bloodlines, and a leader in the reclamation of all people. They have agreed to be married here in Sahael and then rendezvous with their people to travel to Rome. I've sent word to Admiral Abdul who has received reports from 27 ships of your armada so far. He will lead the voyage. The Aardian war is coming, and Rome's help will be needed. Get your Empire in order and the ability to return to Sahael will be simple and open to you."

Ryal and Rashida bowed. They held hands and whispered to each other.

Solomon turned to Abioye.

"The revived Yorubans will help rebuild their section of Khartoum palace. As Emperor of your people, and a king of Sahael, you and your wife are to return to your ancestral homeland of Sahaeland to rebuild. Your son, High King Yinká, will be working with King Onika in the greater matters of the rebuilding of Khartoum and the capital city, and Aarde as a whole. You will return with your people and do your duties in Sahaeland."

"I will do my duty, Solomon," Abioye answered.

"So, if I understand correctly," Aamira interrupted, "we are to leave Sahael and go to Sahaeland? But shouldn't we stay here and wait for Damisiah and Heziara? I haven't even been able to see Oadira yet. I don't want to leave and miss my cousins, especially since I'm starting to get the feeling that you're going to send them off somewhere else too before we can reunite. With the Gates open, can't we travel quickly and easily? I don't understand any of this."

"Once Sahaeland is unified, the two of you will find your way back to Sahael naturally for the sake of all your people," Solomon said, placing his hand on Aamira's shoulder. "Then you will be reunited in glory with your cousins and all the people you love."

Aamira dropped her head and stared at the floor. "I don't want to. Haven't we all given enough?"

"It's not about what we've given." Solomon spoke quietly. "It's about what we've gained. And what we will gain. Trust me when I say that your joy will be full, and these years of separation will feel like but a moment. Such is the promise of Ishtar and Obatala. Do you have faith in them?"

"…Yes," Aamira answered after a thoughtful pause. "My faith has been solidified over the past few years."

Solomon smiled. "Then go joyfully, knowing you will have your heart's desire…just not today."

Electricity flashed from the Nabtahenge Gate, striking the tall ceiling above. A portal swirled in shades of blue and purple. Yinká and Onika stepped out.

"Mother," Yinká grinned as he embraced her. "Solomon told me I won't be seeing you for a while."

Tears filled Aamira's eyes as she looked at her young son, now a man, dressed as the king he was born to be.

"It's time to say your goodbyes," Solomon said.

Lyshyla stepped forward. "We assure you that your youngest son will be safe, and he will be here waiting for your arrival when you return. What of the Demirrians, Solomon?"

"I have sent Vizier Nakhtpaatan to help them get to Sahael, just as I sent you to the Orishans and Adewara to the Yorubans. All is proceeding as best we can guide. Two of the four bloodlines have returned to Sahael. We await the Hausan and the Demirrian bloodlines. Until then, rebuild, lead, and wait for the call. You will only be a few hundred miles to the north but know that you are not to return here until the spirit of Ishtar and Obatala calls to you. You will know it is time with no doubt in your mind."

"I understand," Aamira said.

Solomon turned to the Nabtahenge Gates and waved his arm. The portal's color changed to a deep green with a white center.

"Now it is time for you and your husband to step though, Aamira," Solomon said. "We will send your people in waves over the next few days. Make a plan, follow your wisdom, and trust in each other."

Aamira took Abioye's hand as they stepped toward the light. Electricity tingled her skin and pulled her toward the portal.

They had completed the first stage of their mission. Now there was work to be done and people to save as they waited for the arrival of the third bloodline to Sahael.

THE END

www.ingramcontent.com/pod-product-compliance
Lightning Source LLC
Chambersburg PA
CBHW071425300726
48976CB00004B/1241